CAMPBELL

THE PROBLEM WITH BLISS

by

RICHARD F. WEYAND

RICHARD F. WEYAND

ISBN 978-1-7321280-3-3
Printed in the United States of America

Cover Credits
Model: selfie by Matt Shute
Background: Gang Zhou
Composition by: Oleg Volk
Back Cover Photo: Oleg Volk

Published by Weyand Associates, Inc.
Bloomington, Indiana, USA
October, 2018

CONTENTS

RICHARD F. WEYAND

First Incursion

Captain Tien Jessen, commanding the Commonwealth Space Force destroyer CSS *Whittier*, was not happy.

As the commanding officer of the destroyer squadron's second division, he had inherited squadron command for the time being. The division commander, Senior Captain Jasmine Carruthers, was down sick back on Bliss, and her flagship, the CSS *Knox*, was being commanded by her executive officer.

The squadron's assignment was to protect the precious metal mining operations on Bliss-6c, the third largest moon of one of the system's gas giants. This would normally be an assignment for larger ships, but they were all off practicing maneuvers around Bliss. The Waldheim massacre over a year ago had made planetary commanders more sensitive to the need to periodically drill their commands.

Jessen felt vulnerable, with eight small ships on the other side of the system from the populated planet Bliss-2 and the larger forces for which the destroyers usually acted as pickets. He had made what plans he could, and now it was just sit and wait.

Hopefully nothing would happen before the exercises were over and their normal patrols were re-established.

"Hyperspace transition complete," Duval Space Navy Lieutenant Henry Ambrogi said.

"We're collecting data now, Sir," Lieutenant Commander Debra Hansen said. "We have multiple warships – at least three squadrons – active around Bliss. Hard to make it all out at this distance."

"And what about Bliss-6?" asked Rear Admiral Frank Stenberg, commanding the light cruiser division from his flagship, the DSN *Solar Wind*.

"We have eight ships at standby power levels in orbit around the gas giant, Sir. No class determination possible yet."

"Keep an eye on them, Commander. I want to know what they are as soon as they power up."

"Yes, Sir."

"Let's get under way, Mr. Ambrogi. Division orders. Set course for Bliss-6c at 1.7 gravities."

"Sir, we have a hyperspace transition at zero mark zero-nine-zero on Bliss-6," Lieutenant Theresa Sato said. "Right on the system periphery. Four warships, Outer Colony design. I make them as light cruisers. Beginning acceleration toward Bliss-6 at 1.7 gravities."

"Squadron orders," Jessen said. "Spacing Plan Green-1. Power up per Spacing Plan Green-1 and set course zero mark zero-nine-zero on Bliss-6."

"Spacing Plan Green-1 on course zero mark zero-nine-zero on Bliss-6. Orders transmitted, Sir."

"They've powered up, Sir," Hansen said. "I make it eight destroyers. Coming out to meet us at 1.4 gravities."

"1.4 gravities?" Stenberg asked.

"Yes, Sir. 1.4 gravities."

Stenberg's chief of staff, Captain Maryanne Caro, came up alongside him. "What do you make of that, Sir?"

"I'm not sure what to make of it. If that's really eight destroyers, they have a lot of steel to be coming out after four light cruisers. Then again, nobody ever said the Commonwealth navy was full of faint-hearts. But 1.4 gravities doesn't make any sense. If they're really destroyers."

"You suspect a disguise, Sir?"

"The one thing you can't disguise is acceleration, Maryanne. If they can only make 1.4 gravities, they're not destroyers."

Stenberg considered for a moment.

"Commander Hansen, keep a really close eye on those destroyers. I want to make sure they're what we think they are."

"Yes, Sir."

"We've been under way for half an hour now, Sir," said Commander Sean Medved, Jessen's executive officer.

"That should be long enough. Let's let them see through the disguise a bit. Division orders, Second Division. Begin Option Leak-Through."

"Sir, I've seen some energy anomalies with the Commonwealth destroyers," Hansen said. "Marking them on the plot."

Small red circles appeared around four ships in the oncoming destroyer formation in the plot.

"Those four ships, they've had some power bleed-throughs, Sir. Not destroyer power levels. They're well up into heavy cruiser range."

"Could that be a disguise?" Stenberg asked.

"Unlikely, Sir. Generating a power signature that big from a destroyer, they risk blowing their power plant. Pretty big risk, actually."

"What do you think, Maryanne? A disguise, or is that a division of heavy cruisers with a division of destroyers along for the ride?" Stenberg asked his chief of staff.

"You know, now that those four ships are marked, Sir, that looks suspiciously like a CSF heavy cruiser formation. Look at the separations and the orientation. The destroyers were covering it."

"That's what I think, too. I should have known they wouldn't leave Bliss-6c uncovered for their exercises. Well, higher told me if this wasn't going to be a cakewalk, to come on home and not get ourselves all shot up. I don't consider messing with a division of Commonwealth heavy cruisers to be a cakewalk. Commander Hansen, division orders. Let's flip ship and get out of here."

"Yes, Sir. Orders transmitted."

"They've flipped ship, Sir," Lieutenant Sato said. "They're making for the system periphery."

"Maintain status," Jessen said.

Medved came up alongside Jessen.

"We're pushing our power plants pretty hard, Sir."

"We need to keep it up until they transition, Sean. I don't want them coming back in on us."

"I hope we all hold together."

"That's it, Sir," Lieutenant Sato said. "They've transitioned out of the system."

"Division orders. Stand down Option Leak-Through. Shut down engines. Assess damage. Begin repairs."

"Sir, the *Elmhurst* reports her power plant is failing. They're going to lose it. They're abandoning ship."

"Squadron orders. All ships launch shuttles to assist evacuation of the *Elmhurst*. Let's get our people out of there."

It took over an hour to get everyone off the *Elmhurst*. Somehow the senior chief in the engine control room kept the thing together until they could all get off. He was on the last shuttle to leave, and fifteen minutes later, the *Elmhurst* exploded when her power plant let go.

The *Bennington* had the opposite problem. When they shut the engines down, they couldn't get them restarted. Her poor engines had had enough, and she wasn't going anywhere. They abandoned the *Bennington*, and it continued to drift across the system until it could be retrieved.

The remaining six destroyers of Jasmine Carruthers' squadron returned to station under Jessen's command.

"Go right on in, Captain. She's expecting you," said Lieutenant Commander Rita Allyn, Admiral Mary Rao's secretary.

"Thank you, Commander."

Jessen entered the planetary commander's office at Bliss Fleet HQ.

"Ah, there you are, Captain. Be seated, please."

"Thank you, Ma'am."

"Captain Jessen, I wanted to thank you personally for your actions in response to the recent incursion attempt. The previous two attempts at Bliss-2 were apparently feints to make us think Bliss-6c wasn't their actual target. My exercises, while important to keep us on our toes, left us weakly covered on Bliss-6c. My fault. But your actions nullified my mistake and saved considerable damage to the system's infrastructure. I can't thank you enough."

"Thank you, Ma'am."

"I've characterized your actions as a combat action, so you should receive the Combat Medal and your crews should all receive the Victorious Action ribbon. I also put in for the Distinguished Service Medal for Senior Chief Strnad for holding the *Elmhurst* together while his shipmates got off. That's all up to the Merit Review Board, but I put in for them. I have also characterized the loss of the *Elmhurst* and the *Bennington* as engineering failures after the combat action was over, so there will be no Board of Inquiry into their loss."

"Thank you, Ma'am. That's very kind of you."

"Not at all, Captain. That was a fine piece of work out there. You saw the position you were in – the position I put you in – and came up with a plan to respond in advance of the action. That plan worked, and saved significant lives and infrastructure against a hostile incursion. And in carrying out that plan, you put yourself at risk in ordering the Second Division to run so heavily disguised."

"Only Second Division had practiced that particular option, Ma'am."

"Because, as Second Division commander, you had seen to it that it was part of their repertoire. Yes, Captain, I know. For all those reasons, I have also put you in for the Distinguished Service Medal. It's up to the Merit Review Board, but I don't think they'll have a problem with that one."

"Yes, Ma'am. Thank you, Ma'am."

"You're very welcome, Captain. And thank you again. Dismissed."

En Route

Rear Admiral Jan Childers and her listed companion, Senior Captain Inspector William Campbell, were in Childers' ready room next to the flag bridge on the CSS *Patryk Mazur*. Childers' heavy cruiser squadron had just departed Meili and was on its way to the northern system periphery at zero mark zero-nine-zero on the planet.

"OK, so Meili is done. I think that one went well," Childers said.

"Went well for me, too. The intelligence group here is pretty well buttoned down. It was nice to see such a well run organization."

"As opposed to Natchez."

"As opposed to Natchez." Campbell sighed. "What a waste of resources. We're lucky we haven't had more problems there than I turned up."

"That you know of, anyway. So what's to be done?"

"I sent my report in to Sigurdsen before we left orbit. My guess is Admiral Birken will replace the planetary intelligence chief. And the new guy is going to have to bring in some of his own staff to really get it all cleaned up."

They were one year into the Grand Tour, in which they went from planet to planet, with Jan Childers and her staff training up and drilling the local Commonwealth Space Force squadrons in the standard Fleet Book of Maneuvers. While she did that, Bill Campbell did an assessment of the Intelligence Division's operations in the system. Waldheim, Courtney, Natchez and Meili were done, with Bliss, Hutan, Mountainhome, and Shaanti to go.

Jan Childers at this point was thirty years old and had been in the Commonwealth Space Force for sixteen years. Bill Campbell was thirty-three, and had been in the CSF since graduating the Academy thirteen years before. They had listed themselves as companions with the CSF, which got them consideration in assignments and housing, for the last six years.

"So, Bliss is next. What do we know about Bliss?" Childers asked.

CAMPBELL: THE PROBLEM WITH BLISS

"Well, Bliss has always been pretty quiet, from a CSF point of view," Campbell said. "It's not a big commercial powerhouse. They have increased their deep-space precious metals mining operations significantly over the last ten years, though, and their Outer Colony competitors have been complaining about unfair competition. That's gotten them a little more action lately."

"What kind of action?"

"Three incursion attempts. Local CSF forces ran them off without any actual combat. Didn't get good IDs on the attackers, though."

"I'll be interested to get more details on those when we get there," Childers said.

"Me, too."

"It's three weeks' crossing to Bliss, so I guess we're just going to have to wait to learn more."

The *Patryk Mazur* and her consorts transitioned into hyperspace, and the trip settled into the weeks-long hyperspace transit with which spacers were familiar.

Even at forty-thousand times the speed they could achieve in normal space, interstellar distances were unimaginably huge. The forty-light-year transit from Meili to Bliss would take three weeks in hyperspace, in addition to the time spent spacing to and from the system periphery at either end. Hyperspace travel within the system periphery was not possible, resulting in the destruction of the ship, especially during hyperspace transition. The ship just came apart, like it was being stretched until it literally popped at the seams.

Shipboard life settled into boring routine. The ships maintained one gravity of acceleration throughout the trip, flipping over halfway, so at least there wasn't any weightlessness involved except during the flip. There was lots of free time, though, and the ships' large libraries of virtual reality recordings got extensive use by the crews.

Jan Childers and Bill Campbell, though, were studying up on the situation on Bliss and the reports and personnel files of the senior officers, with Childers concentrating on the line officers of the CSF forces assigned to defend the system, and Campbell concentrating on the Intelligence Division staff officers assigned to the Bliss Planetary Intelligence Headquarters.

Arrival

"Hyperspace transition complete, Ma'am."

"Is our welcoming party here?" Jan Childers asked.

"Yes, Ma'am. CSS *Hannibal* and CSS *Akbar* are standing by at fifteen light-seconds, one-eight-zero mark zero on the ship."

"Send arrival announcement. Navigation Plan Red-2 to twenty miles."

"Ma'am, hyperspace transitions at zero mark zero-nine-zero on the planet, on the system periphery. Distance fifteen light-seconds at zero-mark-zero on the ship. Four contacts. They're warships, Commonwealth design. I make them to be heavy cruisers," Lieutenant Anish Krueger said.

"Admiral Childers. Right on schedule," said Vice Admiral Vina Novotny, commanding her battleship squadron aboard her flagship, the CSS *Hannibal*.

"Yes, Ma'am. We just received their arrival announcement."

"Well, now the fun really starts."

"Hyperspace transition, Ma'am. They've all transitioned out.

"Maintain status."

"Hyperspace transition, Ma'am. The four heavy cruisers are now directly ahead, at zero-mark-zero on the ship, distance twenty miles."

"Well, that's impressive. Launch shuttles."

"They're unfolding cylinders now, Ma'am."

"Get me a comm channel to Admiral Childers."

"Admiral Childers. Welcome to Bliss."

"Thank you, Admiral Novotny. It's good to be here."

"We've launched our shuttles to pick up your passengers."

"We'll clear our shuttle bays and have the passengers ready to go as soon as we can spin up some gravity over here, Admiral. The instructors are all ground-pounders and it'd be no fun getting them aboard in zero-g."

"Understood. I have to tell you, Admiral Childers, we're all looking forward to the training and drills. We've had reasons to believe recently that we need it."

"So I understand, Admiral. I'll be looking forward to meeting you to learn about some of those incidents once the classroom portion is complete and I can get down to Bliss."

"I'll send you the most recent classified reports for your study in the meantime."

"Thank you, Admiral. In the meantime, we have patrol duties and your squadron stands relieved."

"Thank you, Admiral Childers. See you in a couple of weeks then. Novotny out."

Childers' heavy cruisers folded their crew cylinders out perpendicular to the long axis of the ship, and then spun the ships to provide artificial gravity in the crew spaces. Under way, those cylinders folded back parallel to the long axis of the ship, and artificial gravity was provided by the ship's acceleration.

Once spun up, one of the shuttles latched to the racks on the bow of the each ship released and moved away from their ship, opening up a shuttle rack for Novotny's inbound shuttles. The shuttle racks on the bow of the ships were counter-rotated so the racks were stationary.

"I guess I'll see you in a couple of weeks," Bill Campbell said.

"Good luck with your inspection. Hopefully it'll be more like Meili than Natchez," Jan Childers said.

"I hope so, too, but I don't think so. I can already smell something not right here."

"You're thinking of the timing of that last incursion."

"Exactly. The one time they could catch Admiral Rao's forces out of position, and they conveniently show up."

"Could be a coincidence."

Campbell gave her a stern look.

"OK, OK, I forgot. In Intelligence Division, there's no such thing as a coincidence."

"Correct. Someone said something to somebody, and Intelligence didn't know it was going on. And still doesn't suspect anything, if I'm reading those reports right."

"Well, be careful down there," Childers said.

"I'm a pretty hard target, but I can also take some additional measures, and I will."

"Good. Take care of yourself. I love you, and I want you to still be around for a while."

"You, too," Campbell said. "You're the one playing laser tag with beam weapons, after all. I'm just a glorified accountant."

"Yeah. Right. Suspicious bruises on Natchez notwithstanding."

"Like I said, I fell down the stairs. You know how clumsy I am."

Childers snorted.

"Well, be careful on the stairs, then. Love you."

"Love you, too."

Bill Campbell queued with the tactical course instructors headed to Bliss. He was going down to the planet to check in with the chief of planetary intelligence, and to begin his inspection of intelligence operations on the planet. The biggest part of that, on a Commonwealth planet, was counter-intelligence.

During the shuttle trip to the *Hannibal*, he thought back over the reports he had read. No, there was a hole there. Counter-intelligence reports sounded too pat, too "nothing going on, ho-hum."

On Waldheim, on Courtney, on Meili, counter-intelligence was all over their responsibility area. They reviewed mail traffic densities, kept an eye on foreign consulate staff, looked for out-of-the-ordinary off-base relationships. They occasionally found things that were suspicious, looked into them further, sometimes caught someone up to no good. But not on Natchez, and, from the looks of things so far, not on Bliss.

Hell, they didn't even suspect anything after that last incursion.

Not good.

"Shuttle away, Ma'am. All four ships report shuttle departure. Our own shuttles are returning to their racks."

"Good," Jan Childers said. "When we have shuttles aboard, halt spin and fold cylinder. Take us back into hyper and comm Captain Dahl."

"Yes, Ma'am."

Senior Captain Brian Dahl commanded the second division of

Childers' squadron from aboard the CSS *Donal McNee*. They had transitioned out of hyperspace at the southern approach to Bliss, at zero minus zero-nine-zero on the planet.

The Training Division's instructional staff had been distributed across the ships of Childers' squadron so they could take advantage of the limited guest quarters aboard the heavy cruisers. To ground-based staff, even VIP quarters aboard ship were tiny and cramped, but being aboard ship was being aboard ship, and that's just the way it was.

The *Donal McNee* and her division mates had been met at the southern approaches by the CSS *Belisarius* and the CSS *Marlborough*, and transferred their passengers to these two battleships of Admiral Novotny's second division.

"Dahl here."

"Brian, Childers here. Did the transfer go okay on your end?"

"Without incident, Ma'am. All our passengers are on the way to Bliss."

"Excellent. Then I guess it's patrol duty while the training department does its job."

"Yes, Ma'am. Back to work."

Jan laughed. "All right, Brian. Be in touch if you need any help down there."

"You as well, Ma'am. These guys seem to like to come in from the north."

"I'm looking forward to it. Childers out."

The local forces defending Bliss converged on the planet, headed in so their commanding officers, executive officers, and tactical officers could take the two-week classroom training on the standard Fleet Book of Maneuvers, to prepare for the exercises to follow.

On the northern and southern approaches of Bliss, a single heavy cruiser maintained patrol, holding one gravity of acceleration on its patrol route so the crews would have gravity.

Three more heavy cruisers maintained patrol in hyperspace, ready to respond if their pickets reported an incursion.

On Duval, Rear Admiral Frank Stenberg was having an uncomfortable interview with his two-up boss, First Space Lord

Admiral Carla Scola.

"It looks like you got snookered in Bliss," Scola said.

"Yes, it does, but at least I didn't get all shot up. And they ended up losing two destroyers out of the deal, so they really were pushing those disguises a lot harder than anyone would expect," Stenberg said.

"Yes, I think your decision was understandable given the power levels you saw. Still, the political types are pushing hard to get us to do something to disable their precious metals production. They're really hurting us there."

"Well, it's going to have to wait a little while."

"You don't think now is a good time?" Scola asked. "They'll only have a single heavy cruiser squadron guarding the system while they're in training. I would think that would be a good time to get in there and get the job done."

"That's Admiral Childers' squadron you're talking about, so, no, I don't think it's a good time."

"Is she really that good? One heavy cruiser squadron to cover the whole system?"

"I wouldn't attack Bliss right now if we had verified proof all CSF forces had been pulled out of the system and it was being defended by Admiral Childers in a vac suit."

"Really," Scola said.

"Really. Because it would be a trap. The entire asteroid belt would have been replaced with remote control beam mounts, or every freighter in the system would be a Q-ship, or some other crazy ploy you don't expect until it kills you. You never know with her.

"Did you see what she did to the Feirman navy? I watched the sensor recordings, and I still have nightmares about it. She destroyed their entire navy in ten minutes. Her two main forces were in normal space for a couple of minutes apiece. That's it. One minute, the Feirman navy was there, ten minutes later, it was all gone. All of it. And the CSF took no losses. The Feirmians had just enough time to realize she had suckered them before they died.

"Her career is full of stuff like that. Like taking out three heavy cruisers, a light cruiser, and a destroyer in Saarestik with a single heavy cruiser. We don't even know how she did that – none of the Epsley ships survived to tell the tale – but she was the Senior Tactical Officer on that CSF heavy cruiser, and she got the Distinguished

Service Medal for that action, so we know it was her tactical plan. That was just one heavy cruiser, and now she has a whole squadron of them.

"No, it would be easier to just kill all my men and shoot myself. Save all that time and reaction mass spacing out there just to die anyway."

"Wow," Scola said. "Well, you've studied her career, so you would know better than I. She came along after I got promoted out of tactical command. I guess we'll just have to wait until she leaves the system."

"That's my recommendation. If Admiral Childers and I are never in the same star system at the same time, that's just fine with me."

Preparations

On the way to Bliss, alone in his senior guest cabin on the flag bridge of the *Hannibal*, Bill Campbell thumb-swiped the lock on his equipment case, pulled out the electronics sniffer, and turned it on. He meticulously scanned the walls, floor, ceiling, and furniture of the bedroom and adjoining day room, then moved on into the small bath and closet. All clean. There were no electronics in his cabin he didn't expect to be there. He compared the electronic signatures from the door activation unit and the VR sets to the expected values stored in the device, and it indicated they had not been modified.

Campbell took his equipment out of the case, spread it out on the double bed, and inspected it all carefully. He had two sets of the Commonwealth's best body armor for himself and one for Jan, several firearms, together with various holsters, cleaning kits, and accessories, a couple thousand rounds of ammunition, a number of knives, both throwing knives and combat knives, several memory chips containing specialized software, some anti-eavesdropping and anti-snooping electronic devices, motion detectors, minicams and recorders, strapping tape, contact cement, a variety of makeup supplies – all the tools of counter-intelligence.

He inspected each item in turn, and replaced most items in their proper compartments in the equipment case. He didn't know what he would need on this assignment, but you never did. Which is why he inspected everything, thoroughly, every single time.

Campbell stripped down to his skivvies and put on one of the sets of body armor. It was soft and supple but made of an incredibly tough material that would stiffen instantaneously on bullet impact. You would get a hell of a bruise, but no penetration, from a handgun round, and a knife wouldn't penetrate the tough material even in its relaxed state. The material had a limited number of cycles, and he considered one actual bullet impact to be enough to replace the unit, which is why he carried a spare. Just because you'd been shot once didn't mean the job was over.

He selected two carry firearms from the case and loaded them. He put on his uniform shirt, then donned the holsters, one high enough on the calf not to show when he sat down and one under the shoulder. He holstered both firearms and put on the rest of his uniform, then inspected himself critically in the mirror.

He wasn't really expecting any trouble aboard the *Hannibal*. It was much easier to kill someone and get away with it on the planet than it would be shipboard. Everyone's movements and whereabouts were too well known, and the suspect pool too small. But he wanted to get back in practice before they reached Bliss. To work out any kinks in his equipment and get used to wearing it all again after the month-long transit.

Campbell knew there was an active espionage ring on Bliss, and the counter-intelligence unit there was not on top of it. There was no way the timing of that last incursion was just a lucky guess. It was likely both intelligence and operations had been infiltrated. Which meant that espionage ring also knew he was coming, to inspect the intelligence operations. They had three options: be all quiet and hope he missed them, pull out of the system, or take him out before he found and outed them. His experience was they would try the first, and, if that didn't look like it was working, switch to the third. They wouldn't want to pull out an operation that may have taken years to get into place.

He set a motion detector in his cabin, then mounted a camera and synched it to the motion detector. That done, he installed another motion detector and camera in less obvious locations and synched them. Usually, when someone found the first pair, which they were expecting, they wouldn't look for the second. It was just human nature to say, "Ha! Found them," when the real question should be, "Have I found all of them?"

The easiest way to kill someone on a planet and get away with it was to make it look like a mugging. Joy, the capital city of Bliss, wasn't a particularly high-crime city, but it had its share. So one possible plan would be to get him off-base somehow.

Killing him at the Bliss Fleet HQ would also be possible, but present a much more difficult problem. First, it would have to be carried out by CSF personnel or some logged visitor with a reason to be there, not anonymous hired ruffians. Second, most areas of the base would likely be under camera surveillance, at least enough there would be a record of someone's movements if not the actual crime scene.

Subtler methods – poisons, for example – were unlikely, because they were more exotic, less reliable, and detectable after the fact. They screamed that the murder was a hit, and not a random mugging.

Of course, depending on how well they did their background checks on him, someone trying to mug him could end up really surprised. Bill Campbell was accomplished at Enshin, a martial arts form that combined judo and karate and which dated back to pre-space Earth. It was popular in the CSF, being the preferred unarmed combat style with the Navy crowd and taught in the CSF Unarmed Combat School.

Enshin was in fact how he had met Jan Childers nine years ago, sparring in the gym at Sigurdsen Fleet Base on Jablonka. They were well-matched sparring partners, and stayed in practice. Even on this trip, they sparred every other day, as CSF capital ships had Enshin sparring mats in the gymnasium, where the lighter CSF units didn't. In addition, during the long trips between planets, Campbell had sparred on the off days with other ship's crew.

He had never competed for belts in Enshin, preferring to keep his actual level of proficiency rather less well documented, but he figured he was about a second-degree black belt, based on the ease or difficulty he had sparring with opponents who were belted at one level or another. And, a year into the Grand Tour, with one month spacing between planet assignments, he was in practice.

He locked his equipment case down with the rest of his luggage in the small closet and checked the time. He headed out to the officers mess and dinner, activating the motion detectors with a small remote as he left the cabin.

One of Bill Campbell's assets as an operative was his ability to assume the air of an affable, bumbling sort, the kind of person who has been posted into a staff position where he could do little harm and was just idling along his time to retirement.

He was in that mode now, sitting in the officers mess, where he had been invited to sit with a number of senior officers for dinner.

"We know why Admiral Childers is here. What's your mission, Admiral?" Commander Tristan Pascal asked, addressing Campbell as

'Admiral' because there could be only one 'Captain' on ship.

"He couldn't tell you anyway, Tristan. Intelligence Division, after all," Commander Neha Schuler said.

"Oh, no. It's nothing like that," Campbell said with a dismissive wave of his hand. "We just have to have someone from Sigurdsen go out once in a while and make the rounds. Checking the boxes mostly. Stop in, say Hi, see if they need anything that's not showing up in reports, look over the accounting. Hum-drum stuff."

"With an Inspector's badge?" Pascal asked.

Campbell looked down at his uniform, as if surprised to find an Inspector's badge there.

"Oh, that. That's just so I can chat with people without having to go through channels all the time. You know, I can just walk up to somebody and say 'Hi' without having to work through the chain of command. That really gets tedious."

"You sure it doesn't have something to do with the incursion several months back?"

"Oh, there was an incursion? Well, I left Sigurdsen a year ago with eight planets on my schedule, and I'm only half done, so I wouldn't know anything about that. That's Operations, anyway. Not my bailiwick."

"Huh." Pascal didn't seem satisfied with that, but he let it drop and the rest of dinner was uneventful.

Campbell, though, made a mental note to look into the inquisitive Commander Pascal.

Bliss

When the shuttles from the *Hannibal* and the *Belisarius* landed at Bliss Fleet HQ, there was a bus waiting to take the instructional staff to the temporary quarters they had been assigned on base next to the training facility. There was also a ground car waiting, driven by a lieutenant commander wearing Intelligence Division badges. He came up as Campbell exited the shuttle.

"Captain Campbell?"

"Yes, I'm Campbell."

"Lieutenant Commander Kyle Acheson, Sir. I've been assigned to be your aide. Get you anything you need while on base. I can take you to your assigned quarters, Sir."

"Excellent, Commander."

Acheson took Campbell's other two bags while Campbell carried his equipment case. They put them in the trunk of the car, then set off toward Flag Row.

Every CSF base had a Flag Row, an area of townhouses that served as temporary quarters for flag officers on assignment to the base. Senior Captains, with one star, were accommodated on Flag Row as space allowed, and were otherwise housed in Senior Officers Quarters, a notch down in the pecking order. Campbell, though, was companions with Rear Admiral Jan Childers, who would be spending significant time on planet over the next two months, and her priority put them in Flag Row, even if another Senior Captain had to be bumped.

"Rear Admiral Langford would like to meet with you as soon as you have an opportunity, Sir," Acheson said over his shoulder as he drove.

"I had planned on checking in as soon as I settled in a bit."

"And the planetary commander, Admiral Rao, would like you to stop by as well."

"Of course," Campbell said.

"I can make those appointments for you, Sir, whenever you want to set up times."

CAMPBELL: THE PROBLEM WITH BLISS

"What's the local time here, Commander?"

"It's 15:45 right now, Sir," Acheson said.

"How about we set those appointments up for tomorrow morning, then? Admiral Langford first, then Admiral Rao."

"Of course, Sir. I'll see to it and get back to you with times."

"That will be fine."

Campbell looked out the window as they drove across the base. It was all new, yet familiar. Every CSF planetary headquarters looked about the same. Given the whole planet to choose from, and the need for the base to be used for shuttle operations to and from fleet elements in orbit, they were all located in semitropical locations where there was little seasonal variation in the weather. Shuttle operations in snow and ice would have been awful, so the CSF picked its bases to avoid the need.

That usually also put the base near the planetary capital, the early settlers having the same desire for moderate weather given a clean-slate choice. The reduced need for shelter from the weather, allowing more effort and energy to be spent on getting food production under way, made it a lot easier for a new colony to succeed.

So it was on Bliss, with the Bliss Fleet HQ located several miles outside of Joy, the planetary capital.

"Here we are, Sir."

Acheson pulled the car to the curb in front of an anonymous townhouse in a row of anonymous townhouses. The unit number was prominently displayed next to the door of each to assist telling them apart. They retrieved Campbell's luggage from the trunk and walked up the short walk.

"It should open to your swipe, Sir," Acheson said.

Campbell swiped his thumb on the door pad and the door unlocked.

"So far so good," Campbell said.

They walked on into the townhouse, furnished in what Campbell called 'CSF Modern.'

"Yep. CSF-issue flag townhouse, one each," Campbell said.

"Is everything all right, Sir?"

"This is fine, Commander. Is the house a Class 4 secure facility?"

"Yes, Sir," Acheson answered.

"And my assigned office in Intelligence Division?"

"That's a Class 3 secure facility, Sir."

"I'll need a Class 2 workspace, keyed to me only," Campbell said.

"I'll see if I can get that set up, Sir."

"Excellent. Until tomorrow, then, Commander?"

"Yes, Sir. The Officers Mess is just across the street. I'll send you those appointment times, and I'll pick you up in the morning."

"Thank you, Commander."

Acheson saluted and left.

Acheson had left his luggage in the bedroom. Campbell thumb-swiped the lock of his equipment case, pulled out his electronic sniffer, and started scanning the townhouse. Every room, every single square inch. Walls, ceilings, floors, furniture, appliances. Everything.

As a Class 4 secure facility, it should have been scanned before being reassigned. Which, with an active espionage ring on base, meant absolutely nothing.

He found tiny audio pickups in the kitchen, the bedroom, and the living room, plastered into small holes in the wall with a thin coat of paint over them. There was a faint paint smell from the patches, indicating they had been placed recently, within the past week. He also found a video pickup, which was much harder to hide, worked into the decorative pattern on the base of a lamp in the living room and set at forty-five degrees off center, to cover the center of the room.

He pretended not to notice them as he scanned, leaving them in place and continuing his scanning as if he missed them.

Off the kitchen, there was a back exit, likely to meet fire codes more than anything else. He opened the door and checked the lock. It did not respond to his thumb-swipe, so he could not lock or unlock the back door from outside. He looked out the back door and, other than a small stoop, there was no sidewalk, just a small back yard with a board fence around it.

Campbell put the electronic sniffer back in his equipment case and checked the time. Almost 19:00. It had taken three hours to scan the entire townhouse. He walked across the street to the Officers Mess for dinner.

Dinner in the Officers Mess was a solitary affair. Unlike on ship, in which the mess was cramped enough to force camaraderie, the mess on planet was large and spacious, and he ate alone. Left with his thoughts, he considered the way forward.

The people who had bugged the townhouse had done him the favor of giving him several places to start. That they weren't smart enough to realize that the disadvantage of giving him so many avenues of investigation greatly outweighed the likely intelligence value of anything they would get from the pickups was a good sign. They were either not very good at this game, or they were seriously underestimating him. Perhaps they had had free rein here so long, they were simply over-confident.

One obvious line of inquiry was who had sniffed his apartment, and when. Were they a volunteer, or assigned? When had the cleaning been done, and by whom? It should have been done before the sniffing. Was it? If not, who authorized the exception? When had the furniture been changed? Was that lamp new? Where was the furniture inventoried, and who was in charge? Who worked there?

Where was the recorder for those limited-range pickups? Were other townhouses in Flag Row unoccupied at the moment? That was the obvious place to check. They would want to be out of the weather, because, like many tropical locations near the ocean, it rained for about a half-hour every morning here.

On the broader question, who had known about the exercises far enough in advance for the incursion force to assemble and get here? Mail ran on fast courier ships, so it would likely be two weeks transit for the intelligence to get to the other end, another week to assemble a force, and a month's sailing to Bliss from the most likely candidates. Who had known two months in advance of Admiral Rao's plans for exercises?

And espionage is expensive. Getting people to risk their skins for a foreign power required cash. Such rings were usually run out of a foreign consulate. Which consulates had been getting larger-than-usual funding? Which consulate's naval attaché was most friendly with CSF people? Which consulate had the best and most frequent parties, a favorite way of making seemingly innocuous contact with non-consulate folks?

In the meantime, he could try another little trick. See if he was the only person, as required by Class 4 secure facility rules, to have access to his townhouse.

Returning to the townhouse, Campbell surveyed the living room. The couch was under the front windows, with two chairs facing it. He sat on the sofa, looking back into the apartment

"Oh, my. This is kind of dreary. Maybe moving things around would help."

He moved the two chairs to the side walls, and swung the sofa, one end at a time, around to face the windows from the inside wall of the townhouse. He moved the side tables of the sofa from under the windows to the back wall to be on either side of the sofa again.

He sat on the sofa, now facing the windows and the street outside through the opened drapes.

"Well, that's certainly better."

When moving the side tables and the lamps to either side of the now-rotated sofa, the lamps had been rotated 180 degrees as well. The video pickup now faced at forty-five degrees toward the side wall.

And when moving them, Campbell had nicked the edge of the wood base on one of the lamps with his thumbnail. A tiny indention, but it meant he could now tell the two identical lamps apart.

With the video pickup now facing the side wall, Campbell set his own video pickups and motion detectors in the townhouse, and synched them in pairs.

Checking In

Lieutenant Commander Acheson was waiting in the car in front of the townhouse at 07:00, per his mail of the evening before. Campbell's meetings with Rear Admiral Sumit Langford and Admiral Mary Rao were at 08:00 and 10:00 respectively. Campbell had risen at 06:00, and had breakfast in the Officers Mess by the time Acheson arrived.

"Good morning, Sir," Acheson said as he held the rear door of the ground car for Campbell.

"Good morning, Commander. Thank you."

Acheson resumed the driver's seat and they were on their way.

"I thought I would take you to your office first, Sir, if that's all right with you. I'm still working on getting you a Class 2 Secure workspace."

"That's fine, Commander."

They pulled up in front of the Planetary Intelligence Headquarters. Acheson handed the car off to a lieutenant acting as valet this morning and accompanied Campbell into the building. After signing in at the front desk – a requirement for his first trip to the building – they took the elevator to the top floor.

Acheson showed him down the hall to an office on the executive floor.

"This is it, Sir. This is a Class 3 secure office."

Intelligence division regulation office, one each. Yep.

"This is fine, Commander."

"And I'm right next door, Sir, if you need anything. Admiral Langford's office is down the hall, in that direction, and at 09:40 I'll be here to take you to the meeting with Admiral Rao."

"Thank you, Commander. That will be fine."

Acheson let himself out and Campbell put his dispatch bag down on the desk. Sitting down at the desk, he thumb-swiped the terminal and got into his empty local account in the base intelligence system computers. So far, so good.

He withdrew a memory chip from his pocket and inserted it into the terminal. The system ran checks on the software on the chip and pronounced it had passed, which it should, since it was issued by Intelligence Division on Sigurdsen. At the same time, this was a software package not everyone had, to put it mildly. Campbell loaded the software and set it to running, then placed a call to Admiral Rao's secretary.

"Admiral Rao's office. Lieutenant Commander Allyn speaking."

"Commander, this is Captain Campbell. I have an appointment with Admiral Rao at 10:00."

"Yes, Captain. How may I help you?"

"Do you think we could hold that meeting in a Class 1 secure conference room over there?"

"Why, certainly, Captain, if you wish. I'll arrange that for you."

"Thank you, Commander."

The problem was, Bill Campbell knew Mary Rao. Their paths had crossed at Sigurdsen when he was a young lieutenant in the Intelligence Division and she was a captain taking a turn as planetary tactical officer. His dumb-bunny act was going nowhere with her.

At 08:00, Bill Campbell knocked on the office doorframe of the planetary intelligence chief, Rear Admiral Sumit Langford. His door was open.

"Ah, Captain Campbell. Come in, come in. Have a seat."

"Thank you, Sir."

Campbell walked over to Langford's desk, they shook hands, and Campbell sat in one of the two chairs facing the desk.

"Welcome to Bliss, Captain. Did you have a good transit?"

"From Meili? Yes, Sir. Lots of free time. Now it's back to work." Campbell sighed, as if he much preferred the stir-crazy inactivity of a hyperspace transit to being on planet and getting to do his job.

"Yes, though there won't be much work here for you, I'm afraid. Bliss is pretty quiet. Always has been."

My God, does he really believe that? Campbell thought. Aloud he said, "Well, that's good news, Sir. I heard some stuff about incursions and such, and I hoped it wasn't going to be dangerous here."

Langford snorted. "Admiral Rao moved her forces out of position for some fool exercises, and guess what? Some Outer Colony decided to take advantage. They probably had a force sitting out there in hyperspace waiting for an opening, and when one of their freighters transitioned out they told them about it. Rao would have been in serious trouble if not for a destroyer captain who had a lot more guts than brains. As it is, she lost two ships."

"Wow. That's quite a story."

"But that's about it for excitement in Bliss. Admiral Rao is now keeping her ships where they can do the most good, and there hasn't been an incursion since. So not much going on."

"Well, that's good. And I don't mind being lazy when I can." Campbell stifled a yawn. "All this getting up early and running around all the time wears on you."

"But you're here for two months, I understand."

"Well, that's my transportation more than anything. I came into the system with Admiral Childers' squadron, and I'll leave the system with Admiral Childers' squadron, so my schedule is of necessity tied to hers. I don't have two months' of work to do. Not even close."

"Ah, I see," Langford said. "I thought this was going to be a major inspection, what with that two-month timeframe."

"No, nothing like that. It's more of an accounting trip, actually. That's my specialty. Accounting. The rest of the time I'll probably spend on the beach."

"Well, if there's anything I can do to help you while you're here, Captain, please let me know."

"Will do, Sir, but most of my work time will be spent on the computer. When I come into the office, that is."

Back in his office, Bill checked the progress of his software. It had completed its thorough scan of his terminal and account. And the results were pretty much what he figured.

He thought back to the conversation with Langford. The theory the incursion force was waiting in hyperspace for an opportunity, and came in when a freighter told them Rao's forces were out of position, didn't stand scrutiny.

Ships only carried so much reaction mass and supplies. Sitting in hyperspace was going to use lots of both, because you couldn't sit there in zero-g all the time. It was too hard on the crews. So you had to be accelerating on a patrol pattern, usually a big circle, and that used reaction mass. The other option was to sit stationary, spinning the ship for apparent gravity, but that delayed your response time. And the crew is still going to have to eat. After a month's transit to get here, and looking at a month's transit to get back, there wasn't much margin left on reaction mass and supplies even if you doubled up on the ship's container racks.

Of course, you could bring a freighter along for re-supply, but there had been no freighter hyperspace transition sighted out to the sensor limits, and Campbell had never heard of anyone doing resupply in hyperspace. Cargo shuttles didn't have hyperspace generators, for one thing. Leave the envelope of the ship, and poof.

No, he continued to think it was a counter-intelligence failure, and the bugs in his townhouse and the tampering with his terminal and local account confirmed it.

Rear Admiral Langford's chief of staff, Captain Vasia Haber, poked her head into her boss's office.

"Is he going to be any trouble?" she asked.

"Who? Campbell? No, he's a Sigurdsen poof."

"But he's listed companions with Admiral Childers."

"So?"

"She has the reputation of being really competent and smart."

"Well, you know what they say. Opposites attract. The guy's an empty uniform."

At 09:40, Acheson came by to pick up Campbell for his 10:00 with Admiral Rao. They drove over to the Planetary Operations Headquarters in silence, Campbell lost in his thoughts.

"Hello. I'm Captain Campbell. I'm here for my 10:00 appointment with Admiral Rao," Campbell said to the lieutenant commander in the outer office.

"Yes, Captain. Just a moment," Rita Allyn said. She pushed the intercom button on her desk unit. "Ma'am, Captain Campbell is here."

The door to the inner office opened, and Admiral Rao came out into the outer office.

"Admiral Rao. It's good to meet you, Ma'am," Campbell said immediately.

Rao raised an eyebrow but didn't comment. "Rita, can you show us to that Class 1 secure conference room, please?"

26

"Of course, Admiral. This way please."

Allyn led them to the elevators down into the basements. She showed them to a secure conference room, and then departed. Rao and Campbell both thumb-swiped and ran their CSF IDs through a scanner in front of the Marine guarding the door, who checked their faces against his display before he unlocked the door. Once inside, Campbell pulled a small camera from his pocket and photographed the scanning log on the wall before they were seated.

"All right, Captain. You can drop the dummy disguise. I know better. What's going on?"

"Yes, Ma'am. To get right to it, Bliss has an active espionage ring operational here at headquarters. I don't know who's in it yet. About the only thing I can say for sure is you and I aren't part of it."

"I wondered myself, after the incursion during my exercises. But it was more of a hunch. Admiral Langford thinks it was either Murphy's Law or perhaps they were awaiting an opportunity in hyperspace. How are you so sure it's an espionage ring?"

"Well, I wasn't, initially, Ma'am. I mean, that's the first thing I think when I see something like the timing of that incursion. Current Intelligence Division leadership doesn't believe in coincidences, and I find myself inclined in the same direction. I also know enough about ship operations to know that 'hiding in hyperspace' thing isn't as easy as some staff types might think. But they did me the favor of proving it by planting pickups in my supposedly Class 4 secure townhouse and tampering with my Class 3 secure office terminal and local computer account."

"Really. How can they even do that?" Rao asked. "I thought the procedures were designed to prevent that."

"By any single person, yes, Ma'am. By a group of people who control multiple parts of the process, it's possible. It gets harder and harder as you move from Class 4 to Class 1, which is why I think this room might – might, that is – be secure. If not, it will give me a much smaller pool to investigate. It could also have become part of the way things work here. Some people may not even know they're not following procedures. They're simply doing what they've been told to do by higher. It depends on who is involved, and at what level."

"What do you need from me?"

"I need a Class 2 secure workspace, which is basically a Class 1 secure facility with a network connection. I am going to be doing a lot of the investigation by looking at message traffic and the like. I want a Class 2 workspace here, under your control, so I can have some confidence in it. I also asked for a Class 2 secure workspace over in intelligence, and they're having some trouble coming up with one. I think they're trying to figure out how to compromise it before they give it to me."

"OK, that I can do. What else?" Rao asked.

"I need access to your mail log, so I can track the information on the exercises."

"All right. Once you have your secure access and secure account, send me a mail from it and I'll send you an access code. What else?"

"Do you have a twenty-four-hour quick reaction force, either in the Marines or the MPs?" Campbell asked.

"Yes, the MPs have one. We try to get our people out of town before the local police show up when there's trouble during liberty. It's usually spacer on spacer, and we'd rather handle that internally."

"Great. I need a call transponder for them. Full armed response to my location."

"That I can do, too. Anything else?" Rao asked.

"There's one more thing you can do for me, Ma'am. You and I have worked together before. You know my dummy act is a farce. But I need you to help me with it. I have no clue who all is involved in this. It could be Langford, or his deputy, or his chief of staff, or your secretary, or the nice lieutenant commander who's been assigned to me, or some combination of the above. Or it could be none of them. But I need them to think I'm a moron for a while."

"Understood, Captain. I can help there. But once they find out who and what you really are, you're going to be in more than a little danger."

"Then they'll find out I'm more than I seem there as well."

Rao gave him a long appraisal.

"Haven't slowed down in the last ten years?" Rao asked.

"No, Ma'am. Faster than ever."

"All right. But do be careful."

"Yes, Ma'am."

"And, Captain. Bill. It's good to see you again. I don't know how I could be so lucky as to have you show up right now, but I'll take it."

"Yes, Ma'am. We'll get it straightened away."

Rao returned to her office after her meeting with Campbell.

"How did your meeting go, Ma'am?"

"Rita, you know how I've said some Sigurdsen staffers are by nature lazy, stupid, and egocentric?"

"Yes, Ma'am."

"Well, Bill Campbell is exactly the sort I was talking about."

Rao went on into her inner office, shaking her head and muttering.

Getting Started

Admiral Rao didn't run Campbell's requests through her secretary, but contacted the head of the MPs and the IT department directly. When the planetary commander calls you personally with a request, it happens fast.

The result was that, when Campbell got back from lunch at the Officers Mess, he had messages waiting to contact both the head of the Military Police and the head of Operation's IT department. Rather than contact them on his compromised terminal, he walked back over to the Planetary Operations Headquarters where he had met with Rao.

Captain Ramona Karim was in her office when he popped in on her.

"Captain Campbell. Come in."

"Thank you, Captain."

"Here's the screamer you requested."

Karim put a small device out on her desk for Campbell. He picked it up and looked at it. Standard homer/transmitter, about the size of his thumb. It had a cap over the activation button so it wouldn't go off accidentally in your pocket.

"And it's keyed to me, so if I set this off, your team knows who it is?" Campbell asked.

"Yes, absolutely. You said you wanted a full, armed response to your location?"

"That's right."

"What sort of situation are we likely to encounter, Captain?" Karim asked.

"I and any members of my party may be under attack from multiple assailants, either civilian or military."

Karim's eyebrows shot up.

"Military? Members of CSF?" Karim asked.

"Potentially, yes, although I would more expect private citizens. Hired ruffians, actually."

"Armed attack?"

"Potentially. Not necessarily," Campbell said.

"All right. That helps us characterize the threat level."

"We also need to make sure your team doesn't shoot me, as I'm likely to be armed as well."

"We'll make sure our response teams all have seen your photo as the protectee. And the duration?" Karim asked.

"I'll be leaving the system in eight weeks."

"That should be all we need, Captain. Hopefully, you never need to use it."

Campbell next checked in with IT. Captain Varg Ikeda was also in his office.

"Ah, Captain Campbell. Come with me, please."

Ikeda led him to the elevators and down into the secure basements of the Operations headquarters. A Marine stood guard over a short dead-end hallway with perhaps a dozen doors along it. Ikeda and Campbell both thumb-swiped and ran their CSF IDs through a scanner in front of the Marine, who checked their faces against his display.

"Second door on the right, Sirs."

Ikeda and Campbell walked down to the second door on the right, at which point the Marine entered his key into his panel, and pushed the release for that door. The lock cycled, and Ikeda and Campbell went into the office. There was a desk and task chair with a single terminal, and two guest chairs.

Campbell pulled out his small camera and photographed the scanner log on the wall.

"You probably shouldn't have a camera in here at all, Sir," Ikeda said.

"Under my clearance, it's allowed."

Ikeda raised an eyebrow at that, but said nothing more. Campbell surveyed the empty office.

"This is fine, Captain. Thank you," Campbell said.

"And you need this for two months, is that right?"

"Yes. I'm leaving the system in eight weeks."

"All right, then, Sir. I'll leave you to it."

Ikeda left, and Campbell walked over to the desk and set his dispatch bag down on it. He sat down at the terminal and thumb-swiped it, then set his eye to the eyepiece for the retinal scan. The system logged him into a blank secure account for this room. He took a memory chip out of his pocket, loaded the scanner software into the terminal, and set it to scanning.

He pulled out his electronic sniffer and scanned the entire room. It was clean.

Campbell sat back down to the terminal. The scan had completed fast. There was nothing to find. The terminal and the secure account were clean.

He pulled a second chip out of his pocket, loaded the software into the system, and set it to work. He set the timeframe for eight months, three months before the last incursion. This would take a while. The software would be building a map of all the message traffic in Bliss Fleet HQ. He couldn't actually access the mail contents, – not with this software, anyway – but it would map all the message flows.

A third memory chip from his pocket contained an org chart generator. He loaded the software, then logged into the Personnel Division subsystem using an override admin authority from Intelligence Division on Sigurdsen. He set the analyzer to building an org chart from the individual records in everyone's personnel files. This had the advantage of allowing him to backtrack someone's chain of command over time.

He sent a message to Admiral Rao giving her the account number for the secure account. Five minutes later, he got a message from her with an access code to her mail log. He started another process in the mail analyzer to track her mails of the last eight months by message number. That would also take a while.

With those processes running, he headed back over to the Planetary Intelligence Headquarters.

Campbell was sitting in his office, pretending to work on the accounting records for the Intelligence Division, when Lieutenant Commander Acheson appeared at the door.

"Sir? I have that Class 2 secure workspace for you."

"Excellent, Commander." Campbell got up from his desk and grabbed his dispatch bag. "Lead on."

They went down the elevators to the secure basements of the Planetary Intelligence Headquarters, to a hallway similar to that in the

Operations headquarters. They logged in with a Marine there, and were let into an office similar to the one over at Operations.

"Thank you, Commander. This will do nicely."

Acheson left, and Campbell proceeded as before. Setting his scan software running on the terminal, he scanned the entire room with his electronic sniffer. He found one audio bug planted in a wall, as in his townhome. The paint smell of the patch up close was strong. The limited range of the audio pickup meant the recorder was likely in the intelligence headquarters building.

His scanner also found the secure terminal had been tampered with, and the secure account associated with it had been as well. Given the two-stage security of a thumb-swipe and retinal scan, that was pretty impressive, actually. Once this operation was over and everything cleaned up, Sigurdsen should send some IT geniuses out here to figure out how they did that.

Campbell knocked off for the day at that point, leaving a little early. Acheson drove him back to the townhouse. It was only half a mile away, but Campbell wanted to keep Acheson engaged and where he could keep an eye on him.

He thumb-swiped the door pad, and went in. He tossed his dispatch case down on the sofa and sat heavily, as if fatigued by the exertions of a day in the office. He looked over at the lamp on the side table, then over at the other one.

The lamps had been swapped. The video pickup once more covered the center of the room.

On Patrol

The heavy cruisers of Jan's squadron running picket duty on the northern and southern approaches to Bliss accelerated on a patrol pattern, a great circle. The kept under continuous acceleration to maintain apparent gravity in their crew spaces. That circle was partially outside the published system periphery, but most of it was inside the system periphery. At its closest approach to Bliss, though, that patrol pattern remained outside the inner system envelope, the place the CSF knew was the actual limit on hyperspace transitions into and out of the Bliss system. It took two days to space around that circle.

The two ships, one on the northern approaches and one on the southern, were out of synch with each other by one day. In this way, at least one ship was always well inside the published system periphery and immune to surprise attack from hyperspace. Outside the inner system envelope, though, it was in position to make a surprise transition to hyperspace and warn the rest of the squadron, patrolling in hyperspace, of an attack on the system.

Every two days, either ship ended up back outside the published system periphery. When it did, it transitioned into hyperspace and a different heavy cruiser made transition into the system and took picket. Only the flagships did not participate in the picket rotation.

The end result was that mail to the squadron was possible by sending all mail addressed to the squadron to the picket coming up on rotation. It could only be transferred to the squadron in hyperspace once per day, but that was better than no mail at all.

It was on the second day since Bill Campbell should have landed on Bliss that Jan Childers received her first mail from him.

FROM: CAMPBELL
TO: CHILDERS
SUBJECT: ARRIVED SAFELY

CAMPBELL: THE PROBLEM WITH BLISS

Hi, Hon:
I arrived safely on Bliss. Everyone is really nice. Not going to have much to do here. When you come down for planet leave, we'll have some fun. Go hit the beach or something.
Love you.
Bill

Childers read the message again and sighed. That message was completely out of character, which meant Bill knew his local account had been compromised. Everything should therefore be read the opposite. Bliss is not safe, everyone is not nice, he was up to his armpits in work, planet leave would be no fun, and if he hit anything – or anybody – it certainly wouldn't be the beach.

Childers hoped he took care of himself. She didn't know much about what he did, but she had caught whiffs of it over the years. She hoped he wasn't in too deep on this one.

Lines of Inquiry

Wednesday, his second full day on Bliss, Campbell had Acheson drop him off at the Planetary Operations Headquarters, and told him he was done with him for the day. Campbell went down to his secure office in the basement. He checked in with the Marine as before.

His software had completed running overnight, but, before checking on the results of that, he composed a list of his possible lines of inquiry.

1) The spread of knowledge of Rao's upcoming exercises, with particular emphasis on anything more than two months prior to the incursion, which would give time for the incursion to be mounted.

2) The general interconnectedness of people on the base by mail messages, looking for unusual combinations.

3) Consulate parties, consulate funding, consulate contacts from/to CSF personnel.

4) The bugging of his Class 4 secure townhouse. When was it scanned? By whom? Any other logged access?

5) The location of the recorders for the bugs in his townhouse. One of the other townhouses?

6) The swapping of the lamps in his townhouse. When was that done? By whom?

7) The tampering with his Class 3 secure terminal in his office, and his local account.

8) The tampering with the Class 2 secure terminal in the Planetary Intelligence Headquarters.

9) The bugging of the Class 2 secure workspace in the Planetary Intelligence Headquarters.

10) The location of the recorder for the bug in the Class 2 secure workspace. Inside the intelligence building?

It was a long list, but he didn't have to hit on all of them, or even a majority. A single hit could lead him into the web of the group.

At the same time, he had to be careful not to let them know he was doing anything that threatened them. Not until he was ready, anyway.

CAMPBELL: THE PROBLEM WITH BLISS

The risk was that they would implement their bug-out strategy, whatever it was, and the ringleaders would escape the net. He might grab the small fry, but the ringleaders would get away.

And he wanted the ringleaders.

Campbell loaded the videos of his living room and bedroom during the day yesterday. It only went on with motion, so he didn't have to wait long to see what happened. A maid came into the townhouse through the front door, carrying linens and a vacuum cleaner. She put the extra linens in the linen closet in the bedroom and looked for dirty linens in the hamper in the linen closet. She then vacuumed the bedroom.

When she moved to vacuuming the living room, she tried to turn on the lights next to the sofa. She reached up under the shade of one lamp and couldn't find the knob. She looked up under the shade and saw that the knob was on the opposite side from the sofa. She then checked the other lamp, and the knob was also on the other side from the sofa.

She turned off the vacuum, unplugged the lamps, and swapped them. She plugged them in again, turned them on, and vacuumed the room. That done, she turned out the lights, collected her vacuum, and left.

Damn, that was slick, Campbell thought. He still had no idea if the maid had been in on it, if a higher had given her instructions, or if it was pure dumb luck she had reset their video camera for them.

He opened an empty page on the secure terminal, and started generating a suspect list.

Lieutenant Commander Kyle Acheson. What better place to put an inside guy, if you had authority over assignments, than as aide to the Inspector?

Commander Tristan Pascal, the too inquisitive officer aboard the *Hannibal*.

The clueless Rear Admiral Sumit Langford, and any of his immediate staff.

To be fair, Admiral Mary Rao's staff, who certainly had access to the exercise information first.

The maid, and her chain of command in housekeeping.

Whoever assigned the furniture to his townhouse, and his chain of command in housekeeping.

Whoever patches plaster in Flag Row townhouses, and his chain of command, because whoever buried the audio pickups had the exact matching paint.

Whoever swept the townhouse, and his chain of command.

Whoever swept the Class 2 secure workspace, and his chain of command.

The IT guy who set up the terminal in his office, and his chain of command.

The IT guy who set up the secure terminal in the Class 2 secure workspace, and his chain of command.

Whoever patches plaster in the Intelligence headquarters, because whoever buried the audio pickup had the exact matching paint.

Campbell turned to his org chart analyzer. It had built a complete org chart for the Bliss Fleet HQ, including direct reports, temporary assignments, and project assignments, and allowed those to be walked back in time. He marked each of his suspects on the chart, where he knew them, and guessed at the ones he didn't know, marking them in a different color. He rotated the chart around, looking for convergences.

On a hunch, he added registered companions to the chart, and its complexity deepened, with cross-connections between people all over the chart. No fraternization in the chain of command, so none of those connections were vertical, but they were potential connections between chains of command that were otherwise unrelated. He rotated the chart again, looking for convergences of multiple suspect branches into a single thread or node.

He marked some promising connections for future study, then switched to the mail analysis. This diagram was a riot of connections, each marked with the number of mail messages across it. He asked the program to highlight unusual repeated connections. Many of these were in the form of stars, out and back from one person to many in different places in the organization.

There were a number of approved organizations on base that sent out meeting announcements and the like. Duplicate bridge nights, poker games, an astronomy club, clubs for people from various

CAMPBELL: THE PROBLEM WITH BLISS

Commonwealth planets – all the different ways people organized themselves in their personal time. He highlighted each such star in turn, and asked the program to tentatively identify each. The center of the star was usually the contact person listed for the group as the group contact or leader, so that wasn't hard. He marked stars worthy of further investigation and moved on.

Campbell moved on to the analysis of Admiral Rao's mail archive. Most of the mails were to her secretary or chain of command. That's not what he was interested in anyway. He wanted to see where those messages got forwarded.

As expected, Rao's secretary, was a major connection from Rao's office to people all over the CSF operation on Bliss. This was to be expected, and was a pattern he had seen on other planets without Bliss's problems.

He searched Rao's archive for 'exercises', then examined the hits to see which mail was the first to mention the recent exercises. He needed the date. He then went back to the mail analysis to show just the mails from the week after that date.

What Campbell was looking for in all this was low-hanging fruit, something that stuck out to him as unusual. He was relying on his experience of having done similar analyses on planetary headquarters operations before.

But nothing stuck out to him yet. Everything looked like the standard chaos of human interaction within a hierarchy. What he was looking for and did not see was the unusual pattern, the structured piece that didn't fit the chaos. It should tie in with one or more of his suspects.

Maybe this group was more disciplined, and didn't use electronic messaging, but the speed of response in swapping his lamps back made that unlikely.

Clearly more and deeper analysis was needed, but the low-hanging-fruit look-see was first. Sometimes you got lucky.

Campbell checked the time, and walked over to the Officers Mess for lunch.

After lunch he went back to his office in the Planetary Intelligence Headquarters. He was puttering away at some accounting statements when Lieutenant Commander Acheson tapped on the doorframe and walked in.

"Good afternoon, Sir."

"Ah, Commander. There you are. I was looking into clubs on base over at the Planetary Operations Headquarters this morning, and you know what? They have an astronomy club here. Isn't that great?"

"An astronomy club, Sir?"

"Yes. An astronomy club," Campbell said. "I've always liked astronomy. It's one of the reasons I joined the CSF. But planetary staff assignments don't have anything to do with astronomy, and warships don't have windows. Just displays. So it's been an unfilled desire of mine."

"I see, Sir."

"Commander, I was going to ask you. Do any of the consulates here throw parties?"

"Parties, Sir?" Acheson asked.

"Yes, parties. The embassies on Jablonka have the most wonderful parties. Of course, Jezgra's the capital of the Commonwealth, so those are embassies, not consulates. But there's also a lot of brass on Jablonka, so I usually can't manage an invitation. I was wondering if any of the consulates here throw parties like that. As a Senior Captain, maybe I could wangle a few invitations."

"Well, I imagine the consulate parties here are less elaborate affairs than the embassy parties on Jablonka, Sir, but I can look into it."

"Wonderful," Campbell said. "Please do, Commander. Nothing like a few nice parties to lift one's spirits on a boring assignment."

Campbell left early. He told Acheson he was going to walk, stopping by the Officers Mess, which was on the way, for supper.

After supper, Campbell walked over to the Planetary Operations Headquarters and went down to his secure workspace. There was another wrinkle he wanted to look into.

The personnel records for Intelligence Division often had two parts. The unclassified front part included most of the normal personnel data. Rank, years in the service, decorations received, listed companions, if any, pay grade – all that sort of thing. The classified back part included confidential information – like current assignment, training, certifications. In such cases, the front part had the notation

CAMPBELL: THE PROBLEM WITH BLISS

"Other Information Classified" where that information would normally appear. Other Intelligence Division personnel had normal personnel files, without the back part. All their current assignment, training and other information was there on the front page.

But a few people in Intelligence Division had a third wrinkle, the existence of which was itself classified at a high level. Their personnel file was a normal personnel file, without the notation. All the information was there on the front page. Or seemed to be. There was no clue to the existence of the classified back part.

Bill Campbell was one of those few. His personnel file looked completely normal, if rather plebeian. **Rank:** Senior Captain. **Years in Service:** 13. **Current Assignment:** Accounting review of Intelligence Division operations on various planets, per the travel schedule of the CSS *Patryk Mazur*. **Listed Companion:** Jan Childers. **Training:** CSF Academy, with a major in accountancy. **Clearance:** Sensitive.

Yawn.

The hidden, rear portion of his file included things that overrode the false information on the front. **Training:** CSF Academy, Intelligence Track; Unarmed Combat School; Tactical Firearms School I & II; Sniper School; Explosives School; Surveillance Electronics School; Computer Intelligence Methods School. **Certifications:** Unarmed Combat - High Expert; Tactical Firearms - High Expert; Sniper - Expert; Explosives - Expert; Surveillance Electronics - Expert; Computer Intelligence Methods - High Expert. **Specialties:** Infiltration, Counter-Intelligence, Neutralization. **Clearance:** NOT LIMITED.

Whereas for a normal two-part personnel record, access was limited to someone with a Top Secret clearance level, only someone with a NOT LIMITED clearance could see the rear portion of personnel files with a false front. Anyone else querying the personnel database would see the front portion only, with no hint a rear portion existed.

And all those accesses were recorded. That's what Campbell was interested in. Who had accessed his personnel file in the weeks leading up to his arrival, and had anyone accessed the hidden rear portion?

He entered the local copy of the CSF Personnel Division database, pulled up his personnel record, then selected access history. This would not be available to everyone, but it was available to him. He ran it back fourteen months, since before they were assigned on the Grand Tour. This would only show him accesses on Bliss. There were sixteen names listed, including Kyle Acheson, Mary Rao, Sumit Langford, Rita Allyn, and Vasia Haber. Of course, all these people also had a legitimate reason to access his personnel record, but he felt pretty confident one of these sixteen people had to be in the espionage ring.

He pushed into his rear page and selected access history. None. OK, so no one on Bliss had a NOT LIMITED clearance, or, if they did, they were uninterested in one William Campbell. Good.

Campbell isolated each of those sixteen people in the mail diagram, and then highlighted them in combinations, overlapping them in different combinations with the suspects he had highlighted before. Looking for that magic pattern, the one that popped out to his trained intuition, that caught his discerning eye.

He continued working late into the night, walking back to the townhouse about three in the morning. He sent a message to Acheson from his comm that he was under the weather, and not to pick him up that morning. He misspelled 'weather' in that message as 'wether.'

When he got back to the townhouse, he made a lot of noise and staggered as if drunk on his way across the living room. Once out of sight of the visual surveillance, he got ready for bed normally and was asleep within minutes.

A Little Matter Of Death

Bill Campbell got up late the next morning, after a full night's sleep, and had breakfast at the Officers Mess when everyone else was having lunch. A CSF fleet base always had people coming and going that were on different time zones, both from different locations on the planet and from ships arriving. The messes on base always served breakfast around the clock.

He came into the office after lunch.

"Good afternoon, Sir," Acheson said.

"Oh, God. Is it afternoon already? I don't know how those Operations people do it. It must be all that time on ship, standing weird hours on watch."

"Sir?"

"Never drink with an Operations guy, Commander," Campbell said. "They save up all their immunity to alcohol from when they're on ship and can't drink anyway."

"Yes, Sir."

Campbell went down to the Class 2 secure workspace in the Planetary Intelligence Headquarters, the one he knew was compromised. He needed to do some investigation, and his cover in this case would actually serve for that, and might start making people a little anxious without tipping them off as to what he really was and scattering the rats.

People on military bases died at a higher rate than their civilian counterparts in town. Military bases dealt with big machinery, and weapons, and training in all sorts of dangerous activities, and the people who went into the military were also more risk-taking than the general population. The result was a higher mortality rate for a given age.

The CSF maintained a lot of data about this sort of thing, and Personnel Division did a lot of study of the data to try to minimize the effect, but having a lot of risk-taking young people training in dangerous weapons and big equipment all the time was going to result in a certain number of accidents, and that's all there was to it.

Those accidents were costly. In addition to the equipment damage, there was the death payment to the survivors and the loss of invested training in the deceased. Such losses were accounted for, and appeared on the accounting records Campbell, in his cover assignment, was reviewing.

But there was another aspect to accidental deaths. Establishing an espionage ring on a CSF planet often took extreme measures. Someone found out what was going on. Someone was in a position where his subordinate was in the espionage ring, but needed to advance to the next position up to have the access he needed to accomplish the group's goals. In such cases, a fatal accident might be arranged.

Campbell looked up all deaths of CSF personnel on Bliss in the last three years, and compared the death rate per capita to the death rate per capita on other CSF planetary fleet bases. Bliss was toward the top of the range, with three deaths more than the average one might expect.

Going back to the individual deaths, Campbell first stripped out the deaths where the cause of death was listed as disease. He then stripped out the deaths in which the person who died did so as the result of their own actions. He was looking for situations where one person made a mistake, and some other person died. Also deaths due to violence, usually a mugging or rape that occurred off-base.

There were about a dozen such fatalities in the last three years. Again, that number was about three deaths higher than he would expect given the CSF population on-base on Bliss.

He made a mental note to include the people who got promoted as a result of those deaths in his suspect list.

It was time to generate a little concern among the conspirators.

It was late afternoon when Campbell went back up to his office. He buzzed for Acheson.

"Yes, Sir?"

"Commander, the accounting records show costs associated with the deaths of CSF personnel here on Bliss. Those costs, as you may know, are always high. Death benefits, loss of training investment, destroyed equipment – all that sort of thing. One aspect of controlling costs is to get a handle on those things, see if we can't hold those numbers down a bit. So I need some help with this."

"What do you need, Sir?" Acheson asked.

"I think one thing is to go see where each of these deaths occurred. You know, go to the site, talk to the supervisor there, see if I can gain any insight beyond what's in the reports. Do you think we can do that, Commander?"

"I assume so, Sir."

"All right. Good," Campbell said. "A few of those deaths were in town, so I suppose I ought to talk to the Joy Chief of Police, and see if he has any insight for me. We should probably arrange that, too."

"Yes, Sir."

Campbell handed Acheson a note. "These are the dozen or so deaths I'm most interested in, in terms of their circumstances and associated costs. See what you can set up for me along the lines I mentioned."

"Yes, Sir," Acheson said. "Timeframe?"

"Oh, sometime in the next two weeks should be fine."

"Yes, Sir. I'll take care of it."

Campbell left early again, and told Acheson he was heading for the Officers Mess. After dinner, he walked over to the Planetary Operations Headquarters and went down into his Class 2 secure workspace in the basement.

He quickly replicated his earlier work on the local deaths that met his criteria for further investigation. He found the six people who were promoted into positions of authority as a result, and added them to his suspects list.

He then pulled up the mail connectivity diagram and looked at it again, rotating it and highlighting various suspects in combinations. Hmm. Nothing obvious yet. They may have remained disciplined in their communications. Most espionage rings became comfortable as they continued to be undiscovered, and became sloppy.

Campbell tried another tack. Turning someone inside the CSF was sometimes easier if they were originally from the spying nation, and particularly so if they had relatives there who could be threatened or rewarded. He ran a sift over the personnel records for people who were not born on a Commonwealth planet. A large number of people jumped out on the mail diagram. Perhaps fifteen percent. Not unusual, as the CSF was often the easiest way for a new immigrant to get up to speed within the Commonwealth.

What about a further refinement? Bliss had not been a target before it had significantly enhanced its precious metals mining operations. Which Outer Colony planets had the most to lose from that move?

He pulled up an analysis of precious metals mining in the Outer Colonies. Arramond, Duval, Oerwoud, and Wolsey were the big players. They were older than some of the other Outer Colonies, had more investment in system infrastructure and had bigger navies. Duval and Oerwoud were closer to Bliss, while Arramond and Wolsey were on the other side of the Commonwealth. That would be a long reach for an incursion force, making an out-and-back trip without resupply. Then again, some of the Outer Colony worlds had resupply agreements with others.

Sticking with Duval and Oerwoud for the moment, Campbell highlighted personnel who were originally from Duval or Oerwoud on the mail connectivity diagram, then added his suspect list. He rotated the diagram, inspecting it critically. He paid particular attention to companions, as transferred over from the organization chart program. Was that a pattern starting to emerge? He marked some of the more interesting connections.

He checked the time. 02:00.

Well, he was making good progress in assembling things. It was only the end of his third full day on Bliss.

Rear Admiral Jan Childers, aboard the *Patryk Mazur* in hyperspace, got a delayed mail from Bill Campbell.

> **FROM: CAMPBELL**
> **TO: CHILDERS**
> **SUBJECT: BORED**
>
> **Hi, Hon:**
> **End of my third full day here. Nothing to do. Everyone is still very friendly and welcoming. My work is transparent and obvious. Boring! And no hope it will improve soon.**
> **Love you.**
> **Bill**

CAMPBELL: THE PROBLEM WITH BLISS

That was worrisome. Inverting all his sentences as before, the message said 1) he was working wall-to-wall, 2) he had no idea who the threat was, so it could be anyone, 3) he still had no clue what was going on, but 4) he hoped he would be making some progress soon.

Well, no sense worrying about him. He's a big boy and can take care of himself, Childers thought. *I hope.*

Follow the Money

Campbell slept in again on Friday, to get his full eight hours. He had again messaged Acheson not to pick him up this morning. He had breakfast at the Officers Mess and then headed into his office in the Planetary Intelligence Headquarters.

"Good morning, Sir," Acheson said.

"Yes, it's still morning. You see, Commander. I learned my lesson."

"Yes, Sir."

"Have you made any progress in setting up those meetings?" Campbell asked.

"Yes, Sir. I'm setting several up for next week. I'm aiming at the afternoons in order to, uh, accommodate your work schedule."

"Excellent, Commander. Excellent."

"I also thought we would hold the meeting with the chief of police for last, Sir, after you've had the practice of speaking to the others. We probably only get one good bite at that apple, while you can revisit any of the people here on base if you need to ask additional questions."

"Good. Well done, Commander. Carry on."

Campbell stuck with his established routine of leaving early, eating supper at the Officers Mess, and then going to his Class 2 secure workspace in the Planetary Operations Headquarters.

There are several ways to turn someone to working for a foreign power, and one was almost as old as government itself. Money. Tonight he was going to follow the money.

Campbell used his clearance and permissions to extract financial data about his growing suspect list from several sources. Spending at the base commissary. Deposits and withdrawals from the CSF Credit Union. Applications for loans, advances, or assistance submitted through the Personnel Division. What he was particularly looking for were people who were having financial problems, or living at one level, and whose financial situation then dramatically improved. As with the death data, he went back three years.

Getting into the financial data around the privacy protections was cumbersome, and each request had to be made individually. For that, he needed a sign-off at flag rank (senior captain or above) and probable cause. As a senior captain, he was senior enough to sign off on his own access. The issue was, did he have probable cause.

It wasn't something he wanted to screw up, or the perpetrators could be exonerated by exclusion of all subsequent evidence for lack of probable cause. Fruit of the poisoned tree. Any decent defense attorney out of JAG would make that argument whether it was valid or not. That was up to the military court to decide. It was Campbell's job not to make the argument valid.

There was no bulk export of financial data on multiple individuals or across multiple sources, so it took some time. He had to prepare the paperwork for accessing the private financial data for every person in his suspect list and apply his digital signature as both the requester and the flag approval. He saved all those documents in his archive, and copied them to a memory chip from his pocket, then put the memory chip back in his pocket.

When he had all the data collected, he took another memory chip out of his pocket and loaded a new software package into the system. They called this the integrator-visualizer. It would assemble all the data – the financial data, the personnel data, the death data, the planet of origin data, the organization chart, and the mail connectivity data – into one huge chart. He set the software to work on the data he had collected. It would need to run all night for this dataset.

When he finally set that running it was 02:00. He knocked off for the night and walked across the base to his townhouse.

Saturday was nominally a day off from his normal duties, so he donned a plain, midnight-blue shipsuit, the casual wear of choice on base. He had a late-morning breakfast at the Officers Mess and then walked over to the Planetary Intelligence Headquarters.

Campbell was going to try something else today, something he didn't care for much. Of course, all his data research, entry, and organization had been done in virtual reality, or VR. He had surgically embedded implants, with an inductive connection just below the skin on the back of his neck. Contact with the VR transponder in the headrest of the task chair in his Class 2 workspace allowed him to access the terminal completely in VR.

What he had not done yet is use full-immersive VR. He had the full-immersive VR implant kit – sight, sound, smell, touch, hands, locomotion, everything – but he had not used it. Everything had been done using the VR as nothing more than a virtual keyboard and display. To allow his intuition and experience their full reach, though, he needed to use full VR. And he just plain didn't like it.

He got great results with it, he had to admit. There was nothing like being in the data to see the data. And he had to admit there would be no way to work with the huge integrated dataset without it. But he didn't like the loss of control. His perceptions of the real world, and his ability to interact with it – to sense and ward off a physical attack, for example – were diminished almost to zero. It made his skin crawl.

He had been putting it off, but, with his first-stage collection of data complete and the dataset integrated, now was the time.

He had picked Saturday and Sunday for this, because the normal office functions of the base were shut down for the weekend. There would be fewer people in and out of the building today, and he could take one additional precaution. He keyed his account into the thumb scanners on the entrances of the Planetary Operations Headquarters. If one of his suspects swiped into the building, the system would alarm him and he would be out of the VR and back into normal reality well before they could make it to his location.

With that precaution in place, he made the switch to full immersion and entered the integrated dataset in the visualizer portion of the application.

Campbell found himself inside a vast, three-dimensional network of nodes multiply connected by variously colored strands. It went on seemingly forever in all directions, the thousands of nodes each representing a CSF staff member on base. The multi-colored strands were the interconnections, whether mail connections, listed companions, or reporting structure. He could touch any node and see the financial data, planet of origin, and other personnel data for any person. And nodes representing his suspicious deaths on base were highlighted in one color, the nodes of his suspects in another.

He had whole-sphere vision in immersive VR, a trick the brain could be taught once you had full-immersive VR implants, so he saw all the way around, as well as up and down, all in one view.

Campbell lay there and let it all wash into him, paying attention to nothing, allowing his mind to settle into a holistic view of the vast data web without concentrating on anything in particular. He thought of it as soaking in the data. After several minutes, once his mind switched gears and the disturbing view became 'normal' – this wasn't his first time in the visualizer, after all; not by a long shot – he began manipulating the orientation of the data. He selected his suspects and the suspicious deaths, already highlighted, and centered them around himself. The rest of the data pivoted and wheeled about as nodes were pulled this way and that by their interconnectedness until they settled into a new pattern.

It could be a wildly disorienting and nauseating experience, that realignment of the web around his data manipulation, as the data squirmed and wheeled around him, but it no longer bothered him. The key was that initial several minutes of contemplation and opening his mind to the data, soaking it in, and recognizing when his mind had made the switch. Newcomers to the software found out in a hurry that reorienting the data immediately on entering the visualizer was ill-advised. Some never recovered from the experience and could never use the visualizer again without becoming instantly violently ill.

Campbell let the new pattern stabilize, and left himself open to the data, just soaking it in without concentrating on any one thing. After several minutes he highlighted the nodes with non-CSF origins. The web lit up all throughout its volume. He cut that off, and selected only those with Duval or Oerwoud origins, and highlighted them. He considered that view for a while, but no pattern was obvious. He then selected only those with Duval origins, and highlighted them. The highlights were now concentrated where he was, and fewer farther away.

He moved out of the center of his suspects, so he could see his suspect volume from outside. His suspects and the suspicious deaths were highlighted, with the additional highlight of the Duval-born, and he had a clear concentration in his suspect volume. He switched to a highlight of only those with Oerwoud origins, and saw no similar concentration. So, probably Duval, then.

Campbell switched back to those with Duval origins and moved back into his suspect volume. After several minutes, he reached out and grabbed a single strand to highlight it. The highlight spread out through the web, diminishing in intensity where it was not reinforced by the connectivity of the nodes, and increasing in intensity where it was. It faded rather quickly.

He let that strand go and considered, then selected another. This one, in contrast, lit up brightly for a web of connectivity in several directions before fading out. Bingo.

On a hunch, Campbell added an orange-colored highlight for those whose lifestyle or financial situation had taken a significant upward turn. Several of the nodes in his little highlighted web took on an orange hue. He added a blue highlight on suspicious deaths that resulted in the promotion anyone in his highlighted web, and two nodes adjacent to his highlighted web glowed blue.

Campbell froze that view and sat considering it. Soaking it in. That sure looked like a prime candidate for his little espionage ring. It wasn't any proof of anything, however. It was all coincidence and contiguity and connectivity, but not proof. Suspicious as hell, but not proof.

He saved that view, then tried every other strand that connected between or into his suspect pool, but no other strand lit up a web like that. He'd hit it on the second try, a testament to his intuition and visualization skills, but thoroughness had required he try all the others so as not to miss something else, some other, better, link.

Campbell reloaded the saved view and let it settle in his mind again. Everything he had done so far had been without regard to who the nodes represented. Of course, the highlights were his suspect pool and the suspicious deaths to start with, but he had no idea who was in his little highlighted web. Now he reached out to the individual nodes to see who they were.

First, where was the center of the web? Who was the ringleader, at least on base? No doubt the ring was being run by someone in the Duval consulate, but who was the center of the action on base? He considered his little web, then touched a node. Nope. Another. Nope. Hmm. This one? The highlight spread from that node to encompass his little web. OK, so who is that guy? The head of Housekeeping, Commander Vilis Schenk.

What a perfect job for a spy ring leader. You can go anywhere on base and you were anonymous. Not much more than part of the furniture. Put on a coverall, carry a toolbox, and go anywhere. Install audio and video pickups anywhere. Bug furniture, too, like putting a video pickup in a lamp, for example.

Or arrange for a maid to swap the lamps. "Hey, the guy in O-23 is complaining the lamps are hard to turn on and off. He probably rearranged the furniture and doesn't realize the switches on the two lamps are opposite each other. Check it out, and swap the lamps if that'll help." Slick.

Arrange accidents, too, for that matter.

When was he promoted? About two years ago, after the accidental death of the previous head of Housekeeping. How had he died? A scaffold had fallen on him when he was inspecting a work site. Common construction accident, didn't raise any eyebrows. Had the guy who got promoted been there, too? Yup. He had been injured, in fact, as he was on the scaffold when it fell. He twisted his ankle hitting the ground. Pain, but no break. Perfect cover. "Ow, doc. That hurts." Wear a boot for a month, to remind everyone of how close you were to getting seriously hurt, too, then lose the boot. "No, it's been feeling a lot better. Doc says I don't need it anymore."

Who was this person here? Lieutenant Mona Singh, a clerk in Admiral Rao's office. Assistant to her secretary, Lieutenant Commander Rita Allyn. Singh had had some bad financial problems a couple years back, but they were apparently under control now. She had redecorated her apartment recently, by the looks of her commissary purchases. And of course she had access to all the documents circulating around in that office, including plans for the upcoming exercises.

And this person? Lieutenant Christopher Sobol. Night-shift supervisor in the Communications Center. Well, that's how you get messages in and out without detection. Have someone in the Communications Center who can send unlogged 'test messages' when no one else is around. Only two people stand shift in the Communications Center at night. Whenever your underling goes to the necessary or is performing other jobs outside the control room, you do whatever you want.

And this person? The assistant head of counter-intelligence, Commander Veronica Kinley. She headed up all the analysis done in the counter-intelligence department, and was in a position to affect policy in the assessments and advice she gave to her boss. Which no doubt got repeated to Rear Admiral Sumit Langford, the planetary intelligence chief. She's no doubt where the assessment came from that the recent incursion force had probably been laying in wait in hyperspace.

Oh, and she was born on Duval and took the Exam at twenty-one, going straight into CSF Officer Candidate School. She was also the listed companion of Lieutenant Commander Allyn's clerk, Lieutenant Mona Singh, and had also made purchases for their recent remodeling.

She was promoted when the previous assistant head of counter-intelligence on Bliss had been killed in what the police called a mugging gone bad. He was a known party guy – which was a bad hobby for a counter-intelligence agent, unless it was a cover – and had been mugged while out bar-hopping in Joy. He fought back, though drunk, and they had beaten him to death in subduing him.

Or so the police report said.

And this person? Lieutenant Commander Kyle Acheson.

Campbell saved the dataset in this view, then extracted his little web from the greater dataset and saved it as a separate file. He pulled out of the visualizer and full-immersion VR back into normal terminal mode.

There were some countermeasures he could take. One was to log all 'unlogged test messages' in the Communications Center to his secure account. They would still show as unlogged to the Communications Center night operator. Another was to use his override authority to counter the privacy settings on the mail system server and blind copy all mails and messages for his suspects to his secure account. If they kept any kind of communications discipline, he wouldn't pick up much, but if they were going to be sloppy, he'd take it.

Campbell wrapped up the full dataset, with all his notes and the extracted data of his likely spy ring, into a message directly to Vice Admiral Jake Durand, encrypted it, marked it Eyes Only, then re-encrypted it. The listed sender would be this secure terminal account, not his compromised local account, and any return message would come to this terminal only. There was no indication in the message or its header that it came from him, but Durand would know.

It was a month round-tip for fast-courier mail to Jablonka, so he didn't expect anything for a while. But what sending the message meant was that, no matter what happened here on Bliss, Durand would know what was going on. Which was important, because the next steps could get personally dangerous for him. He had no proof. He needed to get the organization to out itself, and the best way to do that was to get them after him.

Once he had proof, he didn't need any orders to go on to the next step. He had standing orders with respect to foreign intelligence operations on Commonwealth soil. Once murder was involved – and he suspected at least those two, the head of Housekeeping and the assistant head of counter-intelligence, were murdered by this ring – his standing orders were clear.

Neutralize.

Campbell's stomach growled and he looked at his watch. 22:00. He had spent ten hours inside the immersive VR. That was one of the things about immersive VR. Since everything you saw, or heard, or felt was supplied by the machine, little things like missing meals went by without notice.

He headed out of the Planetary Operations Headquarters to the Officers Mess, where he ate his supper in solitude while he considered how to proceed.

He could tease them a bit. Make it look like he was stumbling onto what was going on. Maybe get a response. There were the interviews this week with the department heads of those accidental deaths, the two he attributed preliminarily to this group. The department heads there now were the ones who got promoted into place, and whom he suspected of being in on the conspiracy.

He could also make some discreet comments to Acheson, as if he was letting him into his confidence. Get Acheson worked up if nothing else.

Those things might get them communicating, which he was now in a position to intercept, at least if they used CSF channels. If they used civilian channels, Campbell would probably need a court order, and then things got messy.

And Jan was coming up for two weeks of planet leave beginning next weekend. Senior Captain Brian Dahl and the squadron's second division would handle the exercises the first two weeks.

So did he push now, and hope for something to break before Jan came planetside, or wait until after she was gone, back into space to be the hostile force for the second round of exercises? He didn't particularly want things to come to a head while she was on leave. She could be a target of the conspirators as well. Of course, they would probably be surprised there, too.

He hadn't decided what path to take by the time he went back to the townhouse and to bed.

Interviews Begin

Sunday Campbell got up and had breakfast at the Officers Mess, then headed over to the gym. The Enshin sparring area wasn't very busy at the moment, as only the serious types were there. They watched the new guy with the senior captain's badges on his shipsuit come through the gym with some curiosity. He went on into the changing room and came out in gi and plain white belt. He did some warm-ups and then looked for a sparring partner.

None of the more experienced people would spar with him until he had defeated a couple of less skilled people pretty handily. Finally, a young chief petty officer with two knots on his black belt agreed to spar with him.

Campbell initially got him down for the three-count pretty easily.

"Come on, Chief. Do it like you mean it. I'm not fragile."

"As the Captain orders, sir."

Campbell laughed and they set to it. This was much more satisfying, and they split the next four three-counts.

Sitting there cooling off, the chief asked him what his posting was, and Campbell said he was on Bliss temporarily before moving on yet again.

"Must be hard to stay in practice, moving on so often."

"Well, I'm on a heavy cruiser, and she has a sparring area. Admiral Childers and I manage to get in a few three-counts every other day."

"Admiral Jan Childers?"

"Yes. She commands the squadron I'm spacing around with."

"Well, then, that makes me feel pretty good, Sir, to split bouts with you. Never got a chance to spar with the Admiral, but her reputation at Enshin goes way back."

"I can hold my own with her. I have the reach advantage, but she's fast as a snake. She moves faster than you can hit her. But you'd do okay against her."

"Maybe one day. One more go, Sir? Break the tie?"

"Sure, Chief."

The chief took him down, so they were 3-2 after the chief got serious about it, 3-3 including the earlier, tentative bout.

"Not bad for your age, Sir," the chief said.

"Thanks, Chief. I think," Campbell said, and the chief chuckled.

It made Campbell think, though. Maybe he was getting too old for this stuff.

Campbell had lunch in the Officers Mess and then headed over to the Planetary Operations Headquarters. Down in his Class 2 secure workspace, he checked the communications logs on his suspects from the night before. It was the weekend, though, and all was quiet. Then he logged into the Personnel Division database in administrator mode.

He had decided how he was going to proceed. He would string things along until Jan went back up to her ship. She wouldn't take the whole two weeks as uninterrupted planet leave anyway. She'd be up and down a couple of times, and would go back several days early, if prior experience was any guide. And he needed to shake his chaperone for a while.

Campbell pulled out another of his memory sticks, and loaded a new personnel record into the database. Phil Samples. Senior Chief Petty Officer. Mostly maintenance, a lot of it on ship. Transferring here from Meili. Came in on Jan Childers' ship. Personnel transfers hadn't had the priority on the earlier shuttle transfer to the *Hannibal*. Current assignment: awaiting assignment. Solid record. Mostly positive performance appraisals. Couple of black marks. Nothing serious. Couple years to go until his twenty-four-year full retirement, and he wanted to retire on Bliss.

He put Samples in queue for base housing, with a transfer down to the planet toward the end of Jan's leave.

That done, Campbell re-entered his dataset, in the view he had saved, with his suspect pool in the middle of the data. He pondered it a while, letting his mind shift gears, acclimate to the environment. Then he started poking and pulling at connections. Checking connections within the suspect pool. Connections into the suspect pool. He had a couple other possible people, and he concluded some people in the suspect space were probably not involved, before he gave up for the evening.

He had supper in the Officers Mess and made an early night of it.

CAMPBELL: THE PROBLEM WITH BLISS

The next day, Monday, Campbell was up and breakfasted early. He had managed to wave off Acheson picking him up in the mornings, and Acheson wouldn't expect him in until late morning, at best, anyway. He walked over to the Planetary Operations Headquarters and put in a request directly with Admiral Rao for a short meeting at her earliest convenience. He got a quick note back that she would meet him in fifteen minutes in the Class 1 secure conference room they had used earlier.

Campbell was in the conference room when Admiral Rao entered.

"Good morning, Ma'am," Campbell said as he stood.

"Good morning, Captain. What's going on?"

"A short status report, if I may, Ma'am."

Rao sat down at the conference table across from Campbell.

"Proceed, Captain."

Campbell sat down and jumped right into the deep end.

"First, there is in fact a spy ring operating on Bliss. It is being operated for the benefit of the Duval government, probably out of the Duval consulate. They have been reporting your operations status and plans to Duval, for which they have a contact in your office. They have control of Housekeeping, which gives them broad access to facilities across the base and the ability to compromise secure facilities. They also have control over Intelligence Division's counter-intelligence department here, which has lulled Admiral Langford into complacency.

"Second, they have likely committed at least two murders already, to get their people promoted into positions of influence and authority.

"Third, I know who most of the players are, I think, but I don't have any proof yet, just circumstantial evidence. I also haven't nailed down who their consulate contact is. Those will be my next steps."

"And you have a plan for proceeding, Captain?"

"Yes, Ma'am. I'm going to be doing some interviews this week and next, looking into some of the accidental deaths on base over the last couple of years. I'll be trying to nail down exactly who the players are. Then I move on to putting them out of business."

"I will tell you, Captain, I take a rather dim view of murder within my command area, so I want these people."

"Yes, Ma'am. For the record, Admiral Birken and Admiral Durand in Intelligence Division share your sentiment. I won't have specific orders from Sigurdsen for weeks yet, but I have standing orders that pertain to these circumstances. When specific orders come in, I expect them to be – what would you call it? – *very* specific."

"Excellent, Captain. What do you need from me?"

"Well, Ma'am, Jan – Admiral Childers – is going to be down on planet leave in about a week. We will probably take some time off base, do a little sightseeing, some time on the beach, that sort of thing. I now have systems running that will monitor the situation, and we'll see if I get any proof from that. When Jan goes back up to the *Patrick Mazur*, I will go with her, for the two weeks of exercises. And Senior Chief Petty Officer Phil Samples will transfer down to the planet before the *Patrick Mazur* breaks orbit."

Rao's expression tightened as memories flooded back and realization set in.

"Phil Samples rides again, eh?"

"Yes, Ma'am."

"Good."

"I'll attach him to your office, Ma'am. He'll be doing various chores around base, and, whenever questioned, will direct people to inquire of your office. Of your secretary, in particular. She's clear so far, by the way."

"Not a problem, Captain."

"Good. Thank you, Ma'am. I just didn't want you to think nothing was being done."

"Oh, I think with Senior Chief Samples around, things are likely to get done to my satisfaction."

"Yes, Ma'am. Thank you, Ma'am."

"Thank you, Captain." Rao stood up. "And, Captain – Bill – be careful."

"Yes, Ma'am."

Campbell walked over to the Planetary Intelligence Headquarters, arriving in the late morning.

"Good morning, Sir," Acheson said.

"Good morning, Commander."

"The first two of those interviews are this afternoon, Sir."

"Excellent, Commander. Then I should probably go and grab some lunch."

CAMPBELL: THE PROBLEM WITH BLISS

"Yes, Sir."

Acheson drove him to the interviews. The guy had a car assigned to him, and he apparently wanted to use it.

The first interview was in Supply Division. It wasn't with the planetary commander, but with a captain who oversaw the warehouse operations. The death Campbell was investigating occurred when one end of a load broke free of a crane in the receiving warehouse, and the container swung from the still suspended end and hit a chief petty officer supervising the unloading operation. He was killed instantly by blunt force trauma to the head and torso. He had been standing clear of the load, not under it, when it swung to hit him. A fellow spacer had called out to him, and he had tried to evade the container, but had not gotten clear in time.

Campbell asked a lot of questions, then got to his zinger. He asked it just as matter-of-factly as the others.

"Was any thought given to whether this might not have been an accident, but had been a purposeful action by someone?"

The captain responded with some heat. "Why the hell would anyone want to kill Smitty? Meaning no disrespect, Sir. He was the most popular guy in the division. The crane operator was out on disability for three months. He almost had a nervous breakdown, and he can't bring himself to run a crane anymore. Afraid he's gonna kill somebody, and it wasn't even his fault. Cable snapped, and it wasn't halfway through its replacement schedule. Not only did we lose Smitty, I lost the best crane operator I ever had."

"No offense, Captain. It's just a question on this list here. I have to ask."

"Well, you can tell whoever wrote your list that it's a damn fool question, Sir."

"Very well, Captain. Thank you. That's all I had."

The second interview was in shuttle flight training. The department head was a captain who ran the program, turning out the dozens of shuttle pilots a planetary base with four squadrons of deployed warships needed to keep them operational. The death Campbell was investigating was of two spacers who were on staff with the program, a petty officer first class and a seaman second class. The shuttle pilot was nearing the end of training, and was practicing night operations under combat protocols, coming in hot and hard to a landing zone marked out with flares. He lost track of the flares in the wind and rain that night, seeing reflections of the flares on the side of a ground vehicle, and dropped the shuttle right on the vehicle and the two spacers who had set the flares.

Campbell again asked his questions matter-of-factly, including the last one.

"Was any thought given to whether this might not have been an accident, but had been a purposeful action by someone?"

The captain snorted. "Unlikely, Sir. The pilot himself could have been killed, coming down that hard on a ground car. Those shuttles aren't armored. If the ground car hadn't been parked in a bit of a depression he probably would have been. And he didn't get his advanced pilot rating. He's restricted to freight shuttles and daytime ops."

"Ah," Campbell said. "Well, that's all my questions, Captain. Thank you so much for your time."

Acheson was driving Campbell back to Planetary Intelligence Headquarters.

"Did you get what you wanted, Sir? The answers to your questions?" Acheson asked.

"What? Oh. Yes, pretty much."

"Did you get any push-back to that last question, about whether it might not have been an accident?"

"Yes, some. Sometimes staff work means asking uncomfortable questions. Somebody has to do it. It's just my job."

"Yes, Sir."

Campbell left the office early, had supper in the Officers Mess, and then went back over to the Planetary Operations Center. There was still the open question of how they had managed to compromise secure facilities and not be caught by scanner teams.

Scanning for electronic devices in secure facilities was the province of the counter-intelligence group, and he suspected they were already compromised by the assistant group leader. But how do you fake the scanning? That wasn't done by the group leaders, but by other people in the group. It was a boring job, so it was usually rotated among group members. Campbell had done his own time scanning facilities on Sigurdsen, which was one reason he was good at it. But that meant to compromise a facility required an awful lot of people to be involved, or, sooner or later, someone who wasn't part of the spy ring would rotate into scanning and find the bugs.

He ran the name from the scanning log of the compromised Class 2 secure workspace in the Planetary Intelligence Headquarters through the personnel records. Ah, there they were. Assignment: Housekeeping.

Housekeeping? What's with that? He went through the orders coming out of Commander Veronica Kinley, his suspect assistant head of counter-intelligence, searching on 'scanning' and found it. She had delegated 'routine scanning' to Housekeeping, across the whole base. Her group stood ready to assist if they found anything, but otherwise it was left to Housekeeping.

Campbell then went to orders coming out of Vilis Schenk, the head of Housekeeping. He found the order for scanning the various secure facilities on base. There was a schedule attached. He scanned down the schedule. No rotation. The same person scanned the same facilities every time. Well, that solved the rotation problem.

What about Operations? They had their own security group internally that took care of security throughout their facilities on the huge base. And the Military Police reported to Operations. Campbell wasn't sure why that should be. If he were organizing CSF from scratch, that's not how he would do it. But the MPs had always been part of Operations, on every CSF base. Probably a relic of some long-past decision, and it was now tradition, and unquestioned.

The security group within Operations had disagreed with the decision to delegate routine scanning to Housekeeping, and scanned their own secure facilities. Some rare good sense there. He looked at the orders, scanned down the schedule. These routine scannings were done by the Operations security people themselves, and were done on a rotation.

Campbell checked the name on the scanning log of the Class 2 secure workspace he was in. Assignment: Operations Division, Security Group. That checked.

He made an early night of it and headed to the townhouse and to bed.

More Interviews

Campbell was up early and spent most of the morning in the gym. Some of the people in the Enshin area had been there Sunday, so he didn't have to prove himself before sparring with some experienced partners. He had several bouts with a one-knot black belt, winning the series 3-2, before having several bouts with a three-knot black belt, going down 1-4. He was out of practice. He should have been able to hold that to 2-3. Well, that's why he was there.

Campbell had two more interviews on Tuesday afternoon. One concerned a traffic accident involving a couple of spacers who had been running across base in the rain. They ran out from behind a parked truck directly in front of a ground car, which had not been able to stop in time. One was killed and the other injured badly enough to get disability retirement.

In response to his question as to whether or not any thought was given to whether or not it might have been purposeful, the commander he was interviewing was brief.

"I know you're in Intelligence Division, Sir, but sometimes an accident is just an accident."

The other interview concerned two spacers in demolitions school who had neglected the safety rules. One had wired up the detonation wire to the firing switch while his partner finished up wiring the blasting cap. The firing switch end of the wires was always supposed to be disconnected, with a five-foot lightning gap, before wiring up a blasting cap. The deceased had not followed safety regulations, either. The wires being connected to the blasting cap were supposed to be shorted together until the connection was made, to dissipate any charges or currents. When he made the second connection to the blasting cap, it fired, with him sitting virtually on top of the explosive.

In response to Campbell's question as to whether or not any thought was given to whether or not it might have been purposeful, the training instructor was philosophical.

"Some people are just not cut out for certain kinds of training, Sir.

Demolitions School is probably more sensitive in that way than most. We try to recognize those students and weed them out, convince them they should probably not be in this course, but some want to push through anyway. Some of them pull it together and correct their approach. They are some of our best graduates. Others? Well, the field practice is set up so the students can't hurt anyone but themselves, and every couple of years we have a team who just won't learn blow themselves up. It happens."

Tuesday evening Campbell was back in the Planetary Operations Headquarters. How had the spy ring managed to compromise his personal account and the terminal in the Class 2 secure workspace in the Planetary Intelligence Headquarters? He knew generally how it must have been done, with a module between the terminal driver and the security code, but the security code was supposed to check for that.

He logged into the intelligence headquarters system normally and went poking around, looking at the terminal drivers and account settings. Even at his permission level, the terminal drivers were blocked from view, which was not normal. He should be able to see them, though not write them. He invoked sysadmin privileges and looked again. He could see the terminal drivers now, but there was no intermediate code, just the terminal driver.

He logged into the operations headquarters system on another channel. There were the terminal drivers. He compared the terminal drivers. Same size. Same checksum. He did a byte-by-byte compare of the files. They weren't the same. Now that was a cute trick.

Campbell went to full-immersive VR. He entered the saved view of his main dataset. He now lit up all the nodes of anyone with sysadmin privileges in the intelligence headquarters system. Nothing obvious. He touched the node of the head of Housekeeping, let the connection spread. There it was. This guy. Lieutenant Andon Kuang, a computer system administrator. Campbell touched his node, and got a bunch of connections back into his suspect space. Another guy with suspicious recent purchases. And his listed companion was born on Duval, and she had family there. Campbell marked him and saved the view.

Another early night.

CAMPBELL: THE PROBLEM WITH BLISS

Wednesday morning, Campbell went back to the gym. He hadn't gotten too beaten up yesterday, and it was time to start sparring seriously every day in case he needed to be at his best. He found another three-knot black belt who taught him a couple of neat tricks, including one really nice move against one of Jan's favorite attacks. He went down 1-4 again, but a couple of those were close.

Wednesday afternoon, Campbell had an interview with the head of counter-intelligence, in the Planetary Intelligence Headquarters. What were the odds his office wasn't bugged as well? Little to none. He would have to be careful. Dumb-bunny face. If it looked like there was more there, he would have to set up a follow-up meeting somewhere else.

He ran into a contradiction right away.

"Yeah, it was tragic," Senior Captain Bjorn Laterza said. "Not his cup of tea, but going to consulate parties is part of the job when you're in counter-intelligence. My wife and I had a prior engagement that night, so Mike went to that one. Poor bastard never made it back."

"The police report says he was out bar-hopping," Campbell said.

"Mike Chey? Bar-hopping?" Laterza snorted. "No, he wasn't much of a drinker. Hated going to the parties, but he had to take his turn. He sure got into his cups that night, though. Needed to get some air, and took a walk around the block downtown. Normally a pretty safe area, but it wasn't for him. Not that night."

"Was any thought given to whether this might not have been a random incident, but had been a purposeful action by someone?"

"I thought about it, but I don't see how you arrange that. How do you happen to have a consulate party the same night as my wife's garden club event, get my substitute who isn't much of a drinker to overdo it, then just happen to have some toughs waiting for him when he just happens to decide to go for a walk to get some air? Seemed to me an improbable setup."

"Yeah, you're probably right," Campbell said. "Whose consulate was it, anyway?"

"Duval."

Campbell went back to his office.

"How did your interview go, Sir?" Acheson asked.

"Oh, it went well. Another dry hole, but that's what I expected. I'd be surprised to find anything unusual in any of these interviews, actually. But one has to do the work, check the boxes, to be sure."

"Yes, Sir."

Campbell sat in his office and pretended to work spreadsheets as he thought back over the interview. Laterza's chain of coincidence wasn't as thin as he made it sound. How did you arrange for the substitute to go to the party? Simple. Have someone inside the counter-intelligence group check Laterza's calendar to find out when to schedule the consulate party. How do you get the substitute guy to over-drink? Simple again. Spike his drinks.

How do you get him to just happen to go out for a walk? Why, you could suggest to him he doesn't look well, maybe he should get some air. If he doesn't do that, you could offer him a ride home. They found his body down the street and around the corner, but nothing says he got there on his own. The initial contact could have been almost anywhere. They just dropped him at the other end of the block from the consulate so the 'walking around the block for some air' story held together. Hell, they could have bagged him in the restroom and dragged him out the back door of the consulate.

No, it was a setup and murder.

Campbell still needed to figure out who the consulate contact was. That evening he checked the intelligence files on the Duval consulate staff. Apparently these were being kept updated, likely so they didn't look different from other consulate intelligence files.

You have the consul and his wife. The deputy head of mission. The consul's social secretary. The trade development office staff. The passport/visa/migration office staff. The political, economic, and cultural affairs staff. The household staff – those were mostly Bliss natives, except for the butler and the head of the household staff.

No naval attaché. Hmm. He was more used to embassy staff on Jablonka. There was always a naval attaché, and maybe an assistant or two, in an embassy. But that was on Jablonka.

Campbell started with political, economic and cultural affairs. Communication Officer. Could be. Security Coordinator. Definitely could be. What were their profiles like? The Communications Officer was professional staff, had prior postings, either in the Commonwealth or that intelligence knew about from embassy and consulate parties on other planets. The Security Coordinator was a different story. Intelligence Division had no prior postings information on him at all.

He went back through all the non-local staff at the consulate. Every one of them had a back story, a history of embassy and consular assignments, that intelligence knew about. But not the Security Coordinator. What stood out about him was not what they knew about him, but what they didn't know. No priors on him at all. Which meant John Schmitt was most likely an alias.

Ha! John Smith. OK, so he had a sense of humor.

Campbell had some photos of the man, and ran them through facial recognition on the Intelligence Division's files on known Duval foreign service staffers. He got three solid hits, at the 95% level of confidence. Three different names. Three different assignments. Three different planets. That was curious. He dug deeper. They were non-overlapping assignments, so it could all be the same guy.

When did he get to Bliss? Almost four years ago. Well, that fit all the timing parameters Campbell had turned up. Figure a year or more to start turning people, to compromise them enough they were stuck. He could threaten to turn them in, then simply leave the planet on his diplomatic immunity.

Except operating on Bliss under an alias meant he had no diplomatic immunity. He was a spy, and he had conspired in the murder of two CSF officers.

And he wasn't going to get away.

Campbell came into the office late Thursday morning, per the pattern he had established. He had spent all morning at the gym. He was getting his edge back, which he had lost in the reduced sparring time on ship and the reduced variety of sparring partners. Every sparring partner had different moves, different style, different tricks. The best way to hone your edge was to keep changing it up.

"Good morning, Sir," Acheson said as he came into the office.

"Good morning, Commander."

"Two interviews this afternoon, Sir, one in Fleet Maintenance and one in Housekeeping."

"Excellent, Commander."

Acheson drove him over to the Fleet Maintenance Center, which was on the other side of the large shuttle landing field. They had their own portion of the field, because they had so many flight ops to and from ships in orbit, and they maintained their own shuttle fleet. They also performed major repairs at an orbital space dock.

Five members of the facility staff had been killed in a car accident. A group of twelve spacers on liberty had gone up into the mountains south of Joy for a long weekend at a resort. They had rented three cabins, and borrowed a van from base. On the morning of their return, rather than wait for the inevitable morning storm to be over, they had driven back down out of the mountains. That morning storm could bring some pretty heavy rain, especially in the mountains. In one particular downburst, the driver had lost sight of the road and missed a curve. The van went off the road and tumbled down the steep slope. Five of the twelve had been killed when they were thrown from the van as it tumbled. The driver was belted in, and had been one of the seven survivors. Unhurt, in fact. The other six had been ejected behind the rolling van, and not crushed by it, or had managed to remain inside it as it rolled.

The entire department had been shocked by the deaths. With all the dangerous environments and hazardous tasks they dealt with every day, to lose five of their own to something like a car accident seemed, well, unfair. The worst sort of irony. Campbell didn't even ask his last question, about whether this might not have been an accident. Feelings were still too raw about the recent accident, and it was clear it had not been a setup.

The second interview Thursday was in Housekeeping. Commander Vilis Schenk had been promoted from Lieutenant Commander and succeeded Commander Jukai Clark. Clark and Schenk had been inspecting the scaffolding for a recaulk and repaint of the exterior of a building when the scaffolding had collapsed and killed Clark. Schenk himself had been injured.

Campbell asked his last question in a dry, matter-of-fact tone.

"Was any thought given to whether this might not have been an accident, but had been a purposeful action by someone?"

"I don't see who could plan such a thing, Captain. The scaffolding wasn't properly anchored to the building yet. The crew had just gotten it up and broke for lunch. The ultimate mechanism of the collapse was that the legs away from and slightly down slope from the building sank into soil that was softer than expected, and that precipitated the collapse. There was no notice that Jukai and I were going to stop by during lunch to check on progress."

"Ah. I see. And the crew was on lunch break?"

"Yes. They were out on the lawn at the front of the building. No one else was anywhere near the scaffolding, which was along the back wall."

"Very good. Thank you, Commander."

Back in the office, Campbell thought back over the situation with the scaffolding collapse. The crew was all around the front of the building. The back side offices in the building had been emptied for the week to make sure there were no injuries inside the building during repairs. Some tool dropped, which then bounced off the scaffolding and through a window, for example. So there had been no witnesses.

Schenk was a big man, with powerful arms. Clark and Schenk were probably never up on the scaffolding at all. Safety rules would have prohibited it anyway, since it was not yet anchored. One heavy blow to the back of Clark's head with a scaffolding pipe or wrench, then Schenk could just shove the scaffolding over on top of the body. He would then lay out on the ground past the collapse and call for help on his comm. Lucky break he had been thrown clear of the collapsing structure. The sprained ankle was his only injury.

With no witnesses, it was not something that could ever be proved up in court, so Schenk would never be tried for the murder. But espionage was a capital crime under the military code of justice, so Schenk would not escape the firing squad. The 'accident' that killed Commander Jukai Clark had been over two years ago, so it would be justice delayed, but justice would come to Commander Vilis Schenk.

Thursday evening Campbell was back in the Planetary Operations Headquarters. He added the consulate staff to the dataset, and tagged the Security Coordinator. He also pulled in what data the Intelligence Division had on the Security Coordinator's other assignments, under other names. He made sure he had all the other marks and highlights in his view: the mail traffic links, the reporting links, the names of the people scanning the compromised locations, the people with sudden financial upturns, the people with Duval origins or connections. All of it.

Campbell loaded another piece of software from a memory chip. This one, called the Correlation Engine, was relatively new and untried, but he had found it useful. He set the software running in background mode, because it was a resource hog and would tie up the whole machine if he let it. In background mode, it would run at a lower priority than any other user requests.

With that done, he walked back to the townhouse and turned in for the night.

Campbell spent Friday morning at the gym. He now had people asking to spar with him. You learned more from sparring with someone new, as long as he was at or near your own level of ability, than you did sparring with a regular partner. So as a new guy at the two-knot black-belt level or so, he had all the black belts on base hoping for some time with him on the mat.

He got to the office late in the morning, his usual time.

"Good morning, Sir."

"Good morning, Commander. What have you got for me today?"

"The last of the interviews, Sir. With the deputy chief of police for Joy. He's the head of their Homicide Division. We'll need to leave here at 13:00."

"Excellent, Commander. Sounds like I should grab some lunch first."

Campbell looked around with interest as Acheson drove him into Joy. It took them quite a while just to get off the base. Bliss Fleet Headquarters had over two hundred thousand CSF permanently on base, and another two hundred and fifty thousand dependents. He had been spending all his time in the center of the base concentrated around the Planetary Operations and Intelligence Headquarters buildings and their various satellites, like Flag Row and the central Officers Mess.

That said, Joy was the planetary capital of a Commonwealth planet first settled two hundred and seventy-five years ago. Its population of twenty-some million was dwarfed by the cities of Earth, but it was a major city by colony standards.

The downtown was off-center in the urban sprawl, closer to the fleet base – the city had grown up against the sprawling CSF property, then continued to spread in other directions – so they didn't have to drive far into downtown. Acheson was waved to a parking spot that had been reserved for them in the police headquarters parking garage. Acheson accompanied Campbell into the building, but Campbell left him in the outer office when he went in to meet with Demyan Tsukuda, the deputy chief of police.

"Thank you for meeting with me, Chief Tsukuda," Campbell said.

"No problem, Captain. What can I do for you?"

"I had some questions about the murder of one of our spacers."

"Yes, your aide mentioned that. Michael Chey. Is that right?" Tsukuda asked.

"Yes. I'm looking into various deaths of CSF personnel on Bliss over the last several years. Some seem more preventable than others, and that's my focus. I'm something of a loss prevention guy."

"Not drinking so much would be one way to prevent problems. Mr. Chey had a blood alcohol level approaching point-three percent."

"Wow. That's high," Campbell said. "The police report said he was out bar-hopping. That's not quite so, though, am I right?"

"Well, that's what the report says, as you say. But he actually attended a consulate party. We don't like to drag the diplomatic corps into things like that, though. We're concerned about appearances and interstellar implications. So, once the investigation was done, we attributed it to a mugging gone wrong to keep the consulate out of it."

"Ah. I see. Which consulate?"

"Duval," Tsukuda said.

"And the bar-hopping part of it?"

"We were told Mr. Chey had a drinking problem. That he had been a problem at consulate parties before. So saying in the report that he was bar-hopping seemed reasonable, rather than bringing the consulate into it."

"And who told you he had been a problem at consulate parties before?" Campbell asked.

"The consulate security coordinator. John Schmitt."

"OK. Well, that's all my questions, Chief Tsukuda. I appreciate your time."

"No problem, Captain. Glad I could help."

"Commander, is the Duval consulate near hear?" Campbell asked once they were back in the car.

"Yes, Sir. Do you want to go to the consulate?"

"No, I want to go to the other side of the block. To where Chey's body was found."

"Yes, Sir. Is there something you're expecting to see?" Acheson asked.

"The chief said Commander Chey had a blood alcohol level approaching zero-point-three percent. I'm not sure he could have walked very far being that drunk. I want to see."

The diplomatic consulates were in a non-high-rise portion of the city close to a large city park. It was a pretty area. The Duval consulate itself faced the park across the street. Acheson pointed it out as they drove past it, then took a right and another right to go around the block.

"I believe it was right here, Sir. In the middle of the block."

"Right next to that alley?" Campbell asked.

"Yes, Sir. Maybe they jumped him from the alley."

"Could be. OK, Commander, continue around the block."

Acheson made another right, then another. They were back out in front of the Duval consulate, on their right, with the park on their left.

"Not very far," Campbell said.

"No, Sir."

"Yeah, he could probably have walked that, even that drunk. All right, Commander. Let's head back to the base."

Campbell brooded on the way back to Bliss Fleet HQ. No way someone that hammered, who wasn't a big drinker, could have made that walk. But the second time past the front of the Duval consulate, he noted the alley went all the way through the block, right along the consulate garden wall. There was likely a door in that wall, toward the back corner, for taking out the garbage cans or accessing the garage or whatever.

No, they spiked his drinks, bagged him in the consulate, beat him to death in the back corner of the consulate grounds or in the alley, and then dragged his body out the other end of the alley and dumped it on the sidewalk.

They killed him like a mad dog. To get Veronica Kinley promoted. Someone was going to pay for that.

"That's all the interviews, Sir," Acheson said from the driver's seat.

"Excuse me?" asked Campbell, stirred from his thoughts.

"I said, that's all the interviews, Sir. Did you get what you wanted?"

"Oh. Well, I verified there was nothing there. I suppose that's good, right? We know now that these were all accidents or mischance, that there wasn't foul play involved. That was my goal, to know for sure, so I accomplished it. But it's nothing exciting. Just staff work. Checking all the boxes."

When they got back to the Planetary Intelligence Headquarters, it was almost 17:00. Acheson would have dropped him somewhere, but Campbell wanted to stop in at the office and pick up some things. Mostly, he wanted to dump Acheson.

He walked over to the Planetary Operations Headquarters and checked on the status of the correlation engine. It was over half completed. It would probably complete overnight.

He sent a note to Jan from the secure terminal.

> FROM: 2C68B1AB7218890C0483C993C600FDF4
> TO: CHILDERS
> SUBJECT: ARRIVAL?
>
> JC:
> When do you arrive Bliss Fleet HQ?
> WC

Campbell was sitting there contemplating the week's events when the message chime surprised him within twenty minutes.

> FROM: CHILDERS
> TO: 2C68B1AB7218890C0483C993C600FDF4
> SUBJECT: ARRIVAL?

En route. Arrive orbit approx 60 hours. Admiral goes ashore.

That's right. As captain, she had lots to do before she went ashore, but as admiral, she would come ashore to report in right away. So that would be what? Orbit about 07:00 Monday, then the shuttle ride down? Call it 08:30. Reporting in here to Admiral Rao first.

Hmm.

Correlation

On Saturday, Campbell went into the gym after a light breakfast, and either sparred or worked out with weights all morning. He was doing light weights and multiple reps to get the blood flowing, which actually helped his sparring.

After a bigger lunch, Campbell went in to the Planetary Operations Headquarters. The correlation engine had completed over night. He checked the lock on the door, and then went into full-immersive VR.

The visualization of the correlation output was the same as that of the dataset. What the correlation engine did was suppress the uncorrelated elements and rearrange the correlated ones. It also drew in new correlations from the Intelligence Division database. Not just the upper levels of that database, but the highly restricted eyes only data, accessible to his NOT LIMITED security clearance. Even more, the data he had brought along on the Grand Tour, which was only loaded onto the system when you were using it, and only into your own secure account.

All that had been pulled together, and the view had changed. Several conspirators had been added to the view. Also, a number of other suspects had been dropped from the view.

Campbell looked at the correlation histogram. When running a correlation analysis, you got different values of probability for various relationships. The histogram was a chart of the number of relationships at each level of probability. There was usually a dip in this chart. Above this value you had high correlation, or high probability, and those connections were probably meaningful. Then there was a dip. If you set the threshold below the value of the dip, you pulled in all sorts of relationships with low enough probability that you were probably pulling people into the correlation that didn't belong there.

The histogram had a dip at eighty percent or so, but there were a lot of solid correlations running up into the nineties. The selection threshold right now was at eighty percent, as the system defaulted to the bottom of the dip. In Campbell's experience, the bottom of the dip was too low. He moved the threshold up to eighty-five percent, about halfway up the slope out of the dip.

He looked at the dataset now. Three more people in the Housekeeping department. Looking at them, they had come in to the department after the scaffolding accident that killed Jukai Clark. They were replacements for people who transferred out of the department when Vilis Schenk became head of Housekeeping. Two of these three were assigned to perform the security scans on Flag Row townhouses and Intelligence Division offices and secure workspaces. OK, that made sense. What about the third guy? He was the guy who did minor wall repairs, like spackling and touch-up painting and, apparently, planting audio pickups. That being part-time at best, he also took care of furniture in the furnished apartments.

OK, so Clark dies, Schenk takes over, and some people don't care for him. They leave, and he brings in his own people and assigns them the tasks of taking care of bugging interesting places and ignoring bugs they find when scanning. That explained a lot.

Wait a minute. What's this link? One of the guys who left Housekeeping, Lieutenant Christopher Sobol, had been through Comm School. He went over to the Communications Center and became the night guy there, because nobody ever wants third shift. That was one of Campbell's suspects. So one of the guys who left Housekeeping was Schenk's guy, and transferred to the Communications Center under cover of the others leaving. Pretty slick.

What was this batch of links here? Oh, links to John Schmitt's other assignments, under those three other names. But what would link to them?

Schenk did, for one. He was previously posted to Sigurdsen when John Schmitt, under another alias, had been the naval attaché at the Duval embassy on Jablonka. They had thought Schmitt was involved in some incidents at Sigurdsen, and declared him persona non grata in the Commonwealth. And when John Schmitt showed up on Bliss, Schenk transferred here from Sigurdsen. Jukai Clark had been happy to pick up someone with Sigurdsen experience. Poor bastard. It had cost him his life.

Another connection was a weird one. Who was this woman? Petty Officer First Class Susan Todaro. She had also been on the same planet at the same time as one of Schmitt's prior assignments. She was born on Duval. What were these two links? She had been a prior listed companion with Mona Singh, and she had gone to high school on Duval with Veronica Kinley. They actually took the Exam on the same day and became Commonwealth citizens together. Kinley had gone to OCS, but Todaro had come up through the enlisted ranks. What was her current assignment? She was the assistant on third shift at the Communications Center, under Lieutenant Sobol. So Sobol didn't have to wait for his underling to go the necessary or be out of the room when he wanted to do something for the conspiracy. They were both in on it.

And this link? Susan Todaro was listed companions with Lieutenant Andon Kuang, the computer technician who installed the dummy drivers on the secure terminals in the Intelligence Division. He had seen her before, and her Duval origins, when he had found Kuang, but he hadn't tracked back her prior listed companions. Probably a personal blindness there. Campbell had only had one listed companion, and, as far as he was concerned, he hoped it stayed that way. The correlator had looked, though, and found the connection.

Another point there. Usually – not always, but usually – people with same-sex listed companions stuck with same-sex listed companions, and people with opposite-sex listed companions stuck with opposite-sex listed companions, across multiple relationships. People changed listed companions, but they usually stuck with the same sex across different relationships. The true bisexual, who can have a relationship deep enough to list as companions with either sex, was rare, in Campbell's experience. Which suggested Todaro was a Duval plant all the way back to her taking the Exam, and her relationships were a means to an end.

The last link to one of Schmitt's prior assignments was a familiar one. Lieutenant Commander Kyle Acheson.

So it was Schmitt, Schenk, and Todaro who headed up this whole thing. Any of the three could be the ring leader, but it didn't matter.

They were all going down. If he failed, Durand would send someone else. Or a bunch of someone elses.

Campbell saved the current view in the secure account. He wrapped up the full dataset, including the correlation engine results, with all his interview notes, into a message directly to Vice Admiral

Jake Durand, encrypted it, marked it Eyes Only, then re-encrypted it. Once again, the listed sender would be this secure terminal account, not his compromised local account, and any return message would come to this terminal only. He again included no indication in the message or its header that it came from him, but Durand would know.

Campbell spent Sunday morning in the gym, then walked over to the Planetary Operations Headquarters. He opened up the view of the correlation engine results, and just drank it in. How could he take this group down to maximum effect?

First thing, he wanted to nab everybody, and not let any of them get off planet. Schmitt had been a problem before, and would likely turn up again. The same for Schenk and Todaro, who looked like they were career agents for Duval. The other CSF personnel they had subverted were much smaller fish.

A bonus, if he could get it, would be to feed false information into the pipeline. Which meant Schmitt had to be last. He would be the transferor of data to Duval, in the diplomatic pouch, which was actually an encrypted electronic transmission through the mail system. If Campbell could round up the CSF people first, without tipping off Schmitt, then he might be able to give false intelligence to Schmitt that would encourage Duval to do something rash.

Then he would deal with Schmitt.

Rounding up the CSF people on base wouldn't be easy either. They were so interconnected, it almost had to be a simultaneous operation. And he had to get Schmitt's contact before he could transmit to Schmitt that the jig was up. Which meant he had to know who Schmitt's contact was.

The communications taps he had put on the group's communications should turn something up sooner or later, but they were being quiet right now. Maybe Campbell being around had them a little spooked. Enough to get quiet, but not enough to be communicating emergency messages.

All that, and he would like to get Jan off base while she was on planet. He couldn't be sure this wouldn't all blow up while she was here, and he didn't want to be distracted by that threat.

Campbell started looking at resort spots on Bliss. *I mean, you have a whole planet here. There should be some nice places for some* vacation time, right?

He also made an appointment to meet with Admiral Rao the next morning at 08:00, in the Class 1 secure conference room.

Briefing

"Ma'am, I have Captain Jessen for you."

"Excellent. Put him through here, would you, please?"

"Yes, Ma'am."

Childers was in the admiral's ready room next to the flag bridge of the heavy cruiser CSS *Patryk Mazur*, on the way to Bliss orbit. Jessen, by contrast, was in the small captain's ready room on the destroyer CSS *Whittier*, heading out from Bliss for two weeks of exercises against the Red Navy commanded by Senior Captain Brian Dahl aboard the CSS *Donal McNee*. They would, for a time, be near each other as they passed in opposite directions, which would reduce time lags in their conversation.

Jessen's image appeared on the display in Childers' ready room.

"Good morning, Admiral."

"Good morning, Captain. I wanted to talk to you about the last incursion and your role in it. You managed to chase them off, and I thought I would hear directly from you how you did that."

"Yes, Ma'am," Jessen said. "First, I have to admit I'm something of a fan of yours. I've read through *The Science Of Surprise* several times. One of the points that struck me was the idea of exercising your command in maneuvers and strategies that were unexpected, so it would be easier to convince an enemy commander he was seeing something other than what he was actually seeing. One thing you pointed out as particularly useful was the ability to appear to be a ship of a different class."

"Yes, that's right."

"When I was given command of the second division of Captain Carruthers destroyer squadron, I began a program of planning and exercising certain unusual maneuvers, and one of them was pretending to be bigger than we were."

"That's usually pretty easy for one class up or down, Captain," Childers said, "but is much harder for two classes up or down, especially at anything other than extreme range."

"Yes, Ma'am. That's why we practiced. We found we could make the destroyers look like heavy cruisers, even at medium range, if we were willing to take a few chances. For short periods of time, it wasn't a problem, but extended over hours, it would have pretty good odds of destroying the power plant."

"That's a pretty extreme maneuver."

"Yes, Ma'am," Jessen said. "We tucked it away in our bag of tricks and left it there. Then came the exercises. And I found myself with the entire destroyer squadron, because Captain Carruthers was on sick leave planetside."

"But first division had not practiced those maneuvers. Pretending to be heavy cruisers."

"No, Ma'am. So when the incursion came, I had to decide what do we do now. We have Commonwealth civilians and infrastructure to protect, but we have no chance against light cruisers. They have a two light-second reach on us with their beam weapons, and there was no way we could get inside our reach of them before being destroyed. We plotted it to be sure, but by the time we could reach the outer envelope and hyperspace transition, they would already be past us."

"An unenviable position to be in," Childers said.

"Yes, Ma'am. So I thought maybe we could do something unusual to convince the enemy commander he was seeing something other than eight destroyers. Second division pretended to be heavy cruisers pretending to be destroyers. First division acted as our normal destroyer complement. I delayed putting on the disguise as long as I could, to minimize the time we were endangering the power plants, but, in the end, we lost two destroyers anyway. We didn't lose any spacers, thanks to some pretty heroic efforts in the engine room of the Elmhurst, but the ships themselves were junk."

"Why did using that disguise convince the enemy commander, Captain? Why did he fall for it?"

"There were several reasons, I think, Ma'am," Jessen said. "First is that we were coming out to meet him at all. We were obviously a hopelessly outclassed force, but we were not shying from the battle. Now, you know and I know that's the CSF's normal response to a threat to Commonwealth citizens and infrastructure. You fight the battle with what you have. You try to hurt the enemy as badly as you can. Depending on the hostile commander, he may or may not know that.

"Second is that we held our acceleration to 1.4 gravities. We were coming out to meet him, but at heavy cruiser acceleration rates. There's no need to do that with destroyers.

"Third, there were four actual destroyers with us that he could see. Their emissions and ours were distinctly different, because we were pushing those power plants so hard. So we didn't look like the destroyers he could see. He saw two different kinds of ship coming toward him.

"Fourth is that, were those ships destroyers, we would be pushing our power plants so hard as to blow them up or turn them to scrap. Who practices that kind of maneuver such that they could pull it off in a real combat situation?

"Finally, I was relying on the fact that we have more depth than they do. His orders likely included an admonition against taking chances. If he was doubtful about the outcome, go back home in one piece rather than roll the dice."

"Which do you think ruled the day, Captain?"

"I think they all factored in, Ma'am, but I believe four was most important. Who would practice a maneuver sure to destroy his ships if it wasn't done just right, or maybe even if it was? Who would take that risk?"

"Easy answer, Captain," Childers said. "A CSF commander with no choice who had the only force in a position to respond."

"CSS *Zhanshu*. Yes, Ma'am."

Childers raised an eyebrow and Jessen laughed.

"I told you, I'm something of a fan of yours, Ma'am. 'Victory is reserved for those who are willing to pay its price.' "

"As it was, you almost did, Captain. Pay its price, that is."

"Yes, Ma'am. Sun Tzu wasn't kidding. We got lucky. Then again, Seneca wasn't kidding either."

" 'Luck is what happens when preparation meets opportunity.' "

"Yes, Ma'am."

Disclosure

Campbell stopped through the office in the Planetary Intelligence Center early Monday morning. It was just after 07:00, but Acheson was there. Just arriving, apparently.

"Good morning, Sir," Acheson said.

"Good morning, Commander. I just stopped in to tell you I'm taking several days off. My wife is coming down from her ship for planet leave, and we're going to take some time for a trip into the mountains. Get a cabin for a few days. So I won't be needing you until at least Thursday, more likely Friday. Thought I'd let you know."

"Yes, Sir. Thank you, Sir."

"No problem, Commander. See you later."

Campbell walked over to the Planetary Operations Center and went directly to the Class 1 secure conference room in the basement. He was a bit early. Admiral Rao walked in on time.

"Good morning, Captain. More to report?" Rao asked.

"Yes, Ma'am."

"Proceed, Captain."

"Yes, Ma'am." Campbell gathered his thoughts. "I now know with more certainty who the players in this espionage ring are. I still have no evidence to support a conviction, but I hope to turn that up in a couple of weeks. I now know, I think, how the two murders were committed, and who the guilty parties are. Once again, I have no evidence to support a conviction, and, with regard to the murders, I probably never will. But the guilty parties will come up on other capital charges."

"Good," Rao said with satisfaction.

"Yes, Ma'am. I have three goals now. To secure evidence sufficient for a conviction under the CSF military code of justice, to round up all the players without the principals scurrying sway, and, if I can, to feed false information into the pipeline before we round them up."

"Get Duval to do something stupid."

"Yes, Ma'am," Campbell said. "Teaching them a lesson would be good. Not what the diplomats like, perhaps, but CSF has its own priorities."

"As do I, Captain. I like it."

"Yes, Ma'am. Toward that end, you might start talking in your office about holding another set of exercises once the training team and Admiral Childer's squadron have moved on. Make sure they're truly up to snuff. That sort of thing. A repeat of before."

"A repeat, Captain? Leaving Bliss-6 essentially uncovered?"

"Yes, Ma'am. After all, it worked out for us last time. And my understanding is that, after the current training, you can cover Bliss-6 from this side of the system. It could be a nasty surprise."

"I'll be talking to Admiral Childers about that sometime during the next two weeks. If so, then I like the plan."

Rear Admiral Jan Childers got off the shuttle to find that Bill Campbell was not there waiting. Instead, an Operations Division ground car sporting two-star fender flags waited for her.

"Admiral Childers?" the driver, a lieutenant commander, asked.

"Yes, I'm Childers."

"If you would come with me, Ma'am."

"Certainly, Commander. Where are we bound?"

"To a meeting with Admiral Rao, Ma'am."

Jan got into the car for the drive to the Planetary Operations Building. Curiouser and curiouser.

The lieutenant commander parked the car in a reserved spot at the front door, let Childers out of the car, and led her into the building.

"This way, Ma'am."

He led her past the front desk to the elevators, and, once in a car, pushed the button for one of the basements. Childers raised an eyebrow, but made no comment. They walked down a corridor to a Class 1 secure conference room, where she logged in with the Marine on guard.

"Thank you, Commander," Childers said.

"You're welcome, Ma'am."

Rao and Campbell stood when Childers came into the room.

86

CAMPBELL: THE PROBLEM WITH BLISS

"Admiral Childers reporting arrival, Ma'am," Childers said to Rao and saluted. Rao returned her salute.

"Welcome to Bliss Fleet HQ, Admiral Childers. I understand you have a briefing this morning with Captain Campbell here" – she said that with a wink – "otherwise, I'd like to get a briefing from you on the status of your training efforts once Captain Dahl has had a chance to run them around a bit over the next two weeks."

"Certainly, Ma'am."

"All right, then. Admiral, Captain, I'll see you both later."

Rao left.

Childers closed the distance to Campbell in several quick strides and threw her arms around him. As he held her, she spoke into his chest.

"I've been so worried about you. Those messages were scary."

She pulled back and looked up at him.

"What's going on?"

"Sit down. I need to tell you some things."

They sat on the same side of the table, their chairs swiveled toward each other.

"There is an espionage ring here. We were right about that. It has close to a dozen members. They have infiltrated Intelligence Division, including the counter-intelligence and computer operations, Admiral Rao's office, Housekeeping, and the Communications Center. My office is bugged. My terminal is bugged. Our townhouse is bugged. The Class 2 and Class 3 secure spaces in the Planetary Intelligence Headquarters are bugged. And they've murdered at least two people that I know of."

"My God. And you know who they are?" Childers asked.

"I suspect who they are. I think I know. I don't have enough evidence for convictions yet. In the meantime, they know who I am, and who you are. But I've been playing dumb the last two weeks. They may or may not suspect that I'm more than I seem."

"So you can't just arrest them?"

"Not yet," Campbell said.

"But they might kill you?"

"Yes. Or you. Unlikely at the moment, but not impossible. More likely once I poke the hornet's nest. But I'm very difficult to kill."

Childers raised an eyebrow at him.

"It's been tried before," Campbell said, shrugging.

Now both of Childers eyebrows went up, and her eyes grew large. Campbell took a deep breath, and let it out slowly.

"Jan, there are some things I need to tell you. You never had a need to know, and you've been good about not asking. But I need to tell you a little bit about what I do for a living. And after Bliss, I would just as soon you forget it. But right now I need your help."

"Well, you're an intelligence analyst, right? You investigate things, like this spy ring. You use computers and the like and you figure out what's going on."

"Yes, I'm all that. But more than that, I'm what Intelligence Division calls a fixer."

"A fixer?" Childers asked.

"Yes. A fixer. The industry term of art is direct-action operative. Once I do the analysis, once I figure out what's going on, I do what I have to do to fix it. Whatever that is. Sometimes people get arrested. Sometimes people have fatal accidents. Sometimes it's less subtle than an accident. But, whatever it takes, I fix it."

"You kill people."

"If that's the best way to fix it, yes," Campbell said. "Not unlike Bahay, for example."

Several years back, Childers had gone down to Bahay and found and killed four locals who had beaten and raped one of her spacers. It had caused a major dust-up with the planetary commander, Admiral Serge Ludkin, not that Jan had cared.

"That was different," Childers said.

"Yes. On Bahay, you had the moral authority to do what you did, but no actual authority. I have actual authority, from the Defense Minister, through the Chief of Naval Research, through the head of the Intelligence Division. Fix the problem."

"But, Bill, you're putting yourself out there hoping they attack you."

"Yes," Campbell said. "And on Bahay, did you hope the rapists left you alone when you staggered down that road in the dark at 03:00?"

Childers was too honest with herself not to answer truthfully.

"No. I wanted them to attack me so I had an excuse to kill them."

Campbell shrugged, and Childers had to concede his point.

"And you're going to fix Bliss?"

"Oh, yes," Campbell said. "That's part of my standing orders. I suspect, for example, that the Duval intelligence agent running all this out of the Duval consulate is going to have a major, and very public, misfortune. Durand will want to send a message."

"And that's part of your standing orders?"

"Once murder of CSF personnel is involved, yes. I have wide latitude to craft the best response and to carry it out. I may actually get orders back from Sigurdsen – I sent Durand my data and analysis a week ago – but I can't possibly get an answer for another three weeks. In any case, I don't expect them to differ much from what I would do on my own."

"So how can I help?" Childers asked.

"First, I need you to do me a favor."

Campbell pulled his courier bag over on the conference table, and pulled out a set of body armor.

"I need you to wear this whenever you're at Bliss Fleet HQ."

"What is it?"

"Reactive body armor," Campbell said. "Absolutely the best Intelligence Division has. It's made for people with a high likelihood of needing it."

"I thought the best kit were all custom-made. You can't just pull one off the rack and put it on."

"This one was custom-made for you."

Childers looked at him speculatively.

"How long have you been dragging that around with you? How long ago did you have that made?" Childers asked.

"Um, since before we left for Calumet. Six years, give or take. Authorized when we filed as listed companions."

"And never a word."

"You didn't need to know about it until now. Now you do," Campbell said.

"What about you?"

"I'm wearing mine. Have been since the trip in on *Hannibal*."

"So I should put it on –"

"Now would be a good time, yes."

Childers stripped down to bra and panties, and Campbell helped her get into the body armor. He instructed her as she put it on. It covered her torso, the major target for most shooters, like a high-necked dance leotard. It fit perfectly, of course. Regular sparring in Enshin will keep you trim.

"Nice fit," Childers said.

"The armorers in Intelligence Division do a nice job. For the high-end stuff, anyway."

Childers got re-dressed in her uniform. You couldn't tell she was wearing the thin, flexible armor.

"So is that better?"

"Much better," Campbell said. "Now I don't have to worry about you quite so much. Second thing. While you're on the planet, I think we should get off the base. Spend some time on vacation or something. Let the things I've started cooking simmer for a while. Spend some time at a high-end vacation resort or something."

"Can we afford that?"

"No, but Intelligence Division is going to pay for it. We just need to be out of harm's way for a while. Admiral Rao has been completely briefed, so she expects it. And I told my chaperone from the spy ring that we're going to spend several days at a cabin in the mountains. We're actually going to a beach resort instead."

"Can you trust Admiral Rao?" Childers asked.

"Yes. The first really messy op I was on, Mary Rao was a captain, and I was a mere lieutenant. That was just before I met you. So Mary Rao and I have already been through one of these. She couldn't be happier that I'm here."

"And telling your chaperone one thing and doing another? Isn't that suspicious?"

"No," Campbell said. "Husband makes vacation plans. Wife comes home. New vacation plans. Happens all the time."

Childers laughed.

"OK, so then what?"

"Well, I assume you will go up to the ship for a few days next weekend, then come back down and we'll spend some more vacation time somewhere else. While you're gone, I'll stir the pot some more."

"Yeah, I'll probably want to review the first week's exercises with Brian Dahl and work through what to do the second week. Like in the other systems."

"Right," Campbell said. "I expected that. Then you're back on planet for a while and we have a second vacation. Then you go back up to the ship several days before you move out for your phase of the exercises. When you do, I'm going to go along, supposedly to spend the two weeks with you instead of being lonely and bored down here. But one Senior Chief Phil Samples is going to come down to the planet on the last shuttle."

"Which will be you, in disguise."

"Which will be me, in disguise."

"And then you're going to cause trouble."

"Oh, yes," Campbell said. "Lots of trouble. Senior Chief Samples may have to hightail it after that. Which could mean a combat-drop shuttle pick-up somewhere."

"We help Samples escape?"

"No. You arrest him, and take him back to Sigurdsen for trial."

"We don't get back to Sigurdsen for almost a year," Childers said.

"You can't have everything."

"OK, I have the gist of that plan. What else?"

"We can't talk about any of this anywhere else at all. We can't be seen to be meeting here in the Planetary Operations Headquarters, because we don't want them wondering why we need a secure facility to talk or why we think other facilities aren't secure. We need to arrive and leave separately any time we need to talk about any of this. Including today. How long is your shuttle down here?"

"Until I release it, actually," Childers said. "I wasn't sure what your plans were, and I have the admiral's launch, not one of the big shuttles they need for transferring crew down for planet leave."

"Perfect. I'd rather take that to our vacation spot, because the crew of the admiral's launch is less likely to communicate anything about our actual whereabouts to anyone here in Bliss Fleet HQ."

"So who leaves Planet Ops first?"

"Let me go first. I have to pick up my things at the townhouse, and yours are still on the shuttle. Admiral Rao is loaning me that car and driver for the morning, so give me half an hour head start. I'll send the car back to pick you up and meet you at the shuttle pad."

Campbell looked out the launch window through the morning rain at the sprawling Bliss Fleet HQ as they lifted off the pad and gained altitude. Two hundred thousand fleet personnel, and it took less than a dozen people to compromise it all. One could never stay on top of it. *I guess that's what you call job security*, he thought.

Paydirt

They were in an exclusive – a very exclusive – seaside resort several hundred miles from Joy. Or anywhere else, for that matter. A playground for the rich and famous who wanted to get away and not be bothered, the sort of place that didn't publish its prices because, if you had to ask, you couldn't afford it. Security people outnumbered guests by five to one, and it had a spotless reputation for privacy and security. The resort itself had miles of oceanfront beach, about five hundred yards of which were exclusively theirs.

"Oh, I could get used to this," Childers said, sprawled nude on a chaise lounge in the speckled light filtering through the pergola.

"Gonna turn ground-pounder?" Campbell asked.

Childers laughed.

"No. Not yet, anyway. I figure I've got one more good space posting left."

Campbell turned on his side to face her.

"Really? Just one?"

"When we finish this tour, I'll have almost three years as a rear admiral, so vice admiral should be coming up. And vice admiral is still a space posting. After that, full admiral is a ground-pounder job."

"Huh. I never thought you'd give it up. Space in your veins."

"No, it's just the way to get the job done. Kind of hard to serve in a line position in a space navy without being in space."

"And no interest in staff positions."

"Nope. It's necessary – I appreciate good staffers, as you should know – but staff work's not for me. I want to make the command decisions."

"Mmm." Campbell lay back on his chaise lounge. "So, any commands uppermost in your mind right now, Admiral?"

Childers gave him a sidelong glance.

"Just one, Captain."

"My chaise or yours?"

Childers laughed.

On Thursday, in the launch on the way back to Bliss Fleet HQ, Campbell asked Childers about re-staging Admiral Rao's exercises. The admiral's launch from *Patryk Mazur* was secure enough to have that conversation.

"Did you look into the incursion that was made during Admiral Rao's exercises?" Campbell asked.

"Yes," Jan said. "I had a chance to talk with Tien Jessen in a video conference as our ships passed. Turning back that incursion was a near thing. He had a trick up his sleeve, though, and he pulled it out. Not without losing two destroyers, though. No spacers lost because of some pretty heroic efforts by the engine crew of the *Elmhurst*, but that was a near thing, too."

"It was my impression if the same thing had happened after training on the Fleet Book of Maneuvers, it would have been a slam dunk."

"Absolutely. One key part of the strategy is to keep your major combat elements outside the inner envelope, so they can respond in hyperspace anywhere within the system. You don't want your patrols inside the hard system periphery where they're days away from hyperspace capability."

"So if Admiral Rao were to schedule a similar exercise for after we left – "

"The incoming force would get chewed up like doggy biscuits."

"That's all I needed to know."

Late in the afternoon, the shuttle touched down at Bliss Fleet HQ. Campbell got off and headed for the waiting ground car, carrying his bags. Once he was clear, the shuttle spooled up and headed for orbit.

"Did you have a good leave, Sir?" Acheson asked, taking his bags to stow in the trunk.

"Yes, Commander. Wonderful. Back to reality now, though." Campbell sighed. "Back to spreadsheets."

"To the office then, Sir?"

"No, it's too late to really get into anything today. I want to drop my bags at the townhouse before I head over to the Officers Mess."

"Yes, Sir."

After supper, Campbell headed over to the Planetary Operations

Headquarters. He was going to do something he had to be careful about. He'd been thinking about it while on leave with Jan, and it was probably time.

In addition to their work mail accounts, CSF personnel were allowed a personal mail account. While the work mail account was considered CSF property, the personal mail account was a perk of being in the CSF, but not CSF property. There were privacy protections on those mail accounts.

Campbell had already mapped the message flows of his suspects, along with everybody else on base. Now he was going to riffle through the message contents in their work and private mail accounts. For that, he again needed a sign-off at flag rank (senior captain or above) and probable cause. The issue was, again, did he have probable cause.

He entered immersive VR, called up the results from the correlation engine, and let it soak in. He tapped the nodes for John Schmitt, Vilis Schenk, and Susan Todaro. He let the highlight spread across the links to the other conspirators, until the web of his suspect conspiracy was lit up, then froze the view. He selected a two-dimensional representation and watched the visualization squirm and move into the two-d view.

He froze that view, and saved it as Exhibit A. He then had the visualizer prepare the paperwork for accessing the private mail accounts for every person in his web of suspects, applied his digital signature as both the requester and the flag approval, and attached Exhibit A. He saved all those documents in his archive, and copied them to a memory ship from his pocket, then put the memory chip back in his pocket.

Another memory chip contained the mail extraction and analysis software. He loaded it into his secure account, then engaged it over the webbed suspects from inside the visualizer.

The last thing Campbell did was send a secure mail to Admiral Rao.

FROM: 2C68B1AB7218890C0483C993C600FDF4
TO: RAO
SUBJECT: EXERCISES

Best to achieve goals would be to finalize the deployment and schedule for the follow-on exercises Friday. Same deployment as last time, beginning seven weeks from right now.

Seven weeks from now left two weeks for the mail to Duval, one week to get the Duval fleet moving to Bliss and four weeks to get here. And it meant that, as long as Campbell held back for a week or so in doing anything to tip them off, a warning message to the Duval fleet would arrive in Duval after they left.

That done, Campbell headed for the townhouse and to bed.

Friday morning, Campbell was back in the gym. He did quite a bit of stretching this morning, after four days off, so he was loose enough to spar seriously without pulling a muscle or tightening up. He was getting his edge back after all that time on ship, and it felt good.

He puttered with spreadsheets in the afternoon, then knocked off early and went to the Planetary Operations Headquarters. He entered full-immersive VR and opened the visualizer.

The dataset he chose, though, was the extracted mail. One of the things that the extractor prepared was a concordance of all the mail messages. This was a list of all the words in the mails, with the frequency of occurrence. If he selected a word, it would show him a list of all the places it occurred.

Selecting a word would also show him graphically, within the web of his suspects, who used that word in a message, and which direction it went. The link from sender to receiver would glow brighter where it left the node of the sender, depending on how many times the word had been used in that direction.

He didn't expect a treasure trove, and he didn't get one. With professionals like Schmitt involved, they were likely using a message or chat system provided by a third-party outside vendor for anything sensitive. But he needed to check all the boxes. If they wanted to be less professional than he expected, that was OK.

Campbell scanned through the concordance. No occurrences of "exercises." No occurrences of "Duval." No occurrences of "consulate." No communications at all between Schmitt and any of the people inside CSF.

One occurrence of "vacation." What was that about? An exchange between Schenk and Acheson last Tuesday, the day after he and Jan left for the beach resort.

> **Schenk: No activity. What's going on?**
> **Acheson: On vacation. Back by Friday. God forbid he miss his weekend off.**

OK, so Schenk was monitoring the townhouse bugs, and noticed Campbell didn't return to the townhouse on Monday night. And Acheson didn't have a very high opinion of Campbell's work ethic. That was all good.

But without context it wasn't incriminating. And there wasn't much more. He hadn't picked up any other interesting mails among those on his suspect list, and the idea of unlogged test messages hadn't panned out either. They had to be communicating another way.

There was one more thing he could do, now that he had authorized electronic surveillance on his suspect list. He logged into the base communications system as a system administrator. He forked the input/output stream between the base and the civilian networks on Bliss into a filter, filtered for his suspect list, and dumped that to a log file. Let's see if that picked up anything.

He called it quits for the night and walked back to the townhouse.

Saturday morning, after a light breakfast, the gym, and lunch, Campbell went down into the Class 2 secure workspace in the Planetary Operations Headquarters. He wanted to see if his taps had turned anything up.

His fork on the input/output stream off the base, filtered by his suspect list, turned up traffic to and from several people on his suspect list.

Campbell went into full-immersive VR, and used the stream analyzer in the visualizer to separate the streams. He was specifically looking for data to and from Lieutenant Mona Singh, the spy in Admiral Rao's office. If Admiral Rao had finalized her plans for follow-on exercises, that would be something she should communicate.

And there she was. This stream. He selected that stream and opened it. He was looking for the connect and logon sequences, and to see if she was still logged on. He found the connect and logon sequences, and he also found the logoff. Where was she connecting? Bliss Communications Services Corporation, BCSC. He opened the extractor, and prepped it, then he connected to BCSC with her connect and logon sequences.

As soon as Campbell got a connection, the extractor went to work, pulling copies of everything in her message queues, inboxes, outboxes, and archives. It sucked a copy of everything in the account and then logged off. Now, strictly speaking, this wasn't the same as access to CSF computer resources. This was a civilian system, and came under Bliss laws. Strictly speaking, he should have a court order for accessing private computer systems on Bliss.

Except. There was an except here. "Except in cases where the access was made from a CSF computer system or network, and limited to the extent of the access from a CSF computer system or network." In which case, the access rules were the same as for data on CSF computer systems, requiring the flag officer sign-off. That's what the regulations said, and they were approved by the Commonwealth Council as a military necessity. And so he was on solid ground, and would not trigger the improper search and fruit of the poison tree arguments.

If there was any evidence there, that is.

Campbell opened the copy of the account the extractor had made. His heart was racing. Here it was. Was he right, or were these people just trying to form a new club together? A Thursday night card game or something.

Nope, there it was, the transmission of the plans for the upcoming exercises, as well as a reported comment from Admiral Rao: "I'm not worried about another incursion. That was a coincidence unlikely to be repeated. I mean, come on. I'll give you once, but what are the odds of such a coincidence occurring twice?" Nice. Good job, Mary.

He scrolled back up through the archive. There was the transmission of the plans for the previous exercise. He kept scrolling. There was a received message with Senior Captain Bjorn Laterza's calendar for the month Commander Michael Chey was murdered, showing Laterza's wife's garden party event on the evening the consulate later scheduled their party and Chey was murdered when he attended in Laterza's stead.

CAMPBELL: THE PROBLEM WITH BLISS

OK, espionage, accessory to murder, and conspiracy charges against everyone on the receipt list for that email were pretty much a slam dunk.

Who were the players, though? Everyone in this system was using some sort of alias as their login name. He went back through the log of the input/output stream again. He identified the Bliss Fleet HQ system account of each user stream, and who it was registered to, then searched those streams for their BCSC user login names. He got four of them: Singh, Schenk, Acheson, and Sobol.

He would let the tap continue to run, and see if he could get the rest of the aliases. There should be one alias he couldn't get.

John Schmitt would be accessing BCSC through a different connection.

Campbell went to the Officers Mess for supper, then stopped by the gym and watched several people sparring for a while before calling it an early night.

After breakfast, gym, and lunch, Campbell was once again in his Class 2 secure workspace in the basements of the Planetary Operations Center. He entered full-immersive VR and used the stream analyzer to separate the streams again.

He had five more BCSC user login names matched to their CSF identities. Of the ten BCSC user login names in Mona Singh's message boxes, there was only one left unidentified: JS157923.

Campbell snorted. JS. John Schmitt. And Duval's star catalog designation was HD157923.

He sure was a cocky bastard.

He had supper in the Officers Mess and walked back to the townhouse. He pulled his equipment case out of the back of one of the lower kitchen cabinets, from behind the cookie sheets. It was in a canvas carrier shaped to fit it, to disguise what it was. He packed the rest of his things in his bags and got ready for departure in the morning.

The admiral's launch from the *Patryk Mazur* was picking him up tomorrow morning at 08:00.

He sent a message from his comm to Lieutenant Commander Acheson to pick him up at 07:30.

Chameleon

Acheson was waiting with the ground car at the curb at 07:30 when Campbell opened the front door of the townhouse.

"Early start this morning, Sir?" Acheson asked.

"Eh? Oh. No, Admiral Childers is picking me up at the shuttle pad for a little more vacation."

Campbell put his normal two bags out on the stoop, then turned back into the townhouse to get his equipment case. Acheson carried the first two bags to the trunk of the car, Campbell following.

"Another bag this time, Sir?"

"Oh, yes. I'm taking all my paints and colors along. It was so pretty last time, and I had none of my things along. Very frustrating."

"Yes, Sir."

Campbell put the equipment case in the trunk, then got in the rear of the car. Acheson closed the door, resumed the driver's seat, and they headed off.

The admiral's launch from the *Patryk Mazur* settled gently on the shuttle pad and the engines spun down. Campbell and Acheson stood to one side by the ground car, waiting for the pilot to determine it was safe and cycle the hatch. Once the engines had spun down completely, the hatch opened and the steps deployed. Campbell and Acheson walked to the shuttle with Campbell's bags, Campbell carrying his equipment case. The load master came down the steps and took the bags into the launch.

Campbell turned to Acheson.

"Well, Commander, hold down the fort for me."

"Yes, Sir. Have a nice time."

"Thank you, Commander. See you on Friday."

Campbell went on board the launch as Acheson walked back to the car. When everyone was clear, the pilot cycled the hatch and started the engines spinning up. Within minutes they were aloft.

"We need to talk a bit while we're secure here. I need to bring you up to speed on some things," Campbell said.

"I've been wondering how things were going. Go ahead," Childers answered.

"First, I now have my proof. I have enough evidence to convict all of them for espionage, accessory to murder, and conspiracy."

"Those are capital charges."

"Correct," Campbell said. "No imprisonment and parole. I want them to face a firing squad."

"So now what?"

"So now we switch to the rounding-them-all-up stage. But I don't want to do that yet. They just transferred Admiral Rao's plans for a set of follow-on exercises after we've left the system. I left enough time in the scheduling for the information to get to Duval, for them to get their incursion force together, and for them to get here during the exercises. What I need to do now, though, is wait long enough before rounding them up that the fleet will have departed Duval before a follow-up message can get to them."

"What about the guy at the Duval consulate?" Childers asked.

"He'll be last. In the meantime, you need to work with Admiral Rao to have the exercises play out so the arriving Duval forces think they're good to go in on Bliss-6c, but get their clocks cleaned instead. Write up a tactical plan or something. Whatever you call it."

"That's easy. I've reviewed the sensor recordings, and I spoke with Captain Jessen, so I know what happened. No problem dealing with a repeat performance of that. We can build in some options, depending on what they do. Maybe some things to convince them they caught us with our pants down."

"Excellent," Campbell said. "OK. Well, with all that taken care of, we can enjoy our vacation."

"Back to the beach?"

"Yeah. The mountains are cool and all that, but all in all I'd rather just lie around naked on the beach."

"Works for me."

The resort was as secure, the food as good, the beach as beautiful, and the weather as perfect as the prior week. After the daily morning shower, the sky cleared and the sun came out for the rest of the day. Warm but not hot days, cool nights, soft breezes. The beach faced west, and the sunsets were incredible.

On the morning of their last day, Childers watched Campbell rummaging in his equipment case.

"Whatcha looking for?" she asked.

"Ah. Here they are," Campbell said.

He took an electrocast out of its pouch and rolled it up his right forearm and around the elbow. He positioned it just so and then connected the controller and applied the voltage. The cast hardened over the course of a minute or so. He disconnected the controller and put it back in the case. Withdrawing a sling from the case, he put the sling over his head and put his right arm in the sling.

"What do you think?" Campbell asked.

"More misdirection?"

"Of course. An excuse to go up to the ship with you. Given my demonstrated lack of work ethic, this is more than enough excuse for me to blow off the next two weeks on planet and go up to the ship. And it will mean they know I am out of action."

Childers just shook her head.

"You sure you're not overdoing it?" she asked.

"No. You never are, until you get bit. Haven't gotten bit yet. People believe what they want to believe."

It was mid-morning on Friday when the admiral's launch touched down gently on the shuttle pad at Bliss Fleet HQ. An admiral's launch always touched down gently. The people who assigned pilots in the CSF had learned long ago that an admiral's complaints carried a lot more weight than anybody else's.

Acheson was waiting with the ground car. He walked up as the hatch cycled and the steps extended. The load master handed out Campbell's two bags to Acheson. Then Childers and Campbell walked down the steps.

Acheson saluted Childers and she returned it. Campbell didn't, his right arm in the sling and his uniform jacket just pulled over his shoulder without the arm being in the sleeve.

"Admiral. Captain." Then, "What happened to your arm, Sir?"

"I slipped on the wet veranda after the rain. It was terrible, Commander. I didn't get a chance to do any drawing or painting at all."

CAMPBELL: THE PROBLEM WITH BLISS

Childers couldn't believe the bit of whiny tone in Campbell's voice. It was subtle, but way out of character for the Bill Campbell she knew. He was playing the Sigurdsen desk pilot perfectly.

"That's too bad, Sir. Are you bringing your art supplies then?"

"No, Commander. I can't use them anyway for a month. At least. They're just going to take them up to the ship when they go back."

"Ah. I see, Sir."

Acheson stowed their bags in the trunk, then saw them both seated in the back of the car. He took the driver's seat and spoke over his shoulder.

"Where to, Ma'am?"

"Planetary Operations Headquarters for me," Childers said.

"And then I suppose we should head over to the Planetary Intelligence Headquarters."

"Yes, Ma'am," Acheson said, giving precedence in address to the higher-ranking of the two.

They dropped Childers off at the Planetary Operations Headquarters, and then headed on to the Planetary Intelligence Center.

Rear Admiral Jan Childers was meeting with Admiral Rao in a Class 1 secure conference room in the basement of the Planetary Operations Headquarters.

"So you don't think we will have any trouble dealing with a similar incursion if they try it this time, Admiral?" Rao asked.

"No, Ma'am. A critical component of the strategy is that combat elements on patrol remain in the outer envelope, where transition to hyperspace is always available. Those elements can maneuver in hyperspace to the location of the incursion and emerge into normal space either behind or in front of the hostile force. In the previous exercises, your combat elements were maneuvering well inside the outer envelope, and they were too far from the outer envelope to provide timely relief to Captain Jessen's overpowered force."

"Well, the simplest response to a similar incursion is to have the defenders actually be what they only appeared to be in the prior incursion: four heavy cruisers and four destroyers. Try to inspire a 'You can't fool me with the same trick' response. But that is also the most obvious ploy to anticipate for someone thinking it through rather than following their gut-level response."

"Correct, Ma'am," Childers said. "So I have a few wrinkles that should prove to the hostile commander that what he is seeing is what is actually there, while mounting the response from another quarter."

"A 'watch this shiny object over here, pay no attention to my other hand' strategy?"

"Yes, Ma'am."

"Oh, I like that," Rao said. "Do tell me more, Admiral."

"Damn!" Campbell said.

Acheson appeared in the doorway.

"Is something wrong, Sir?" he asked.

"This isn't working, Commander. I can't type, I can't select columns of numbers, I can't scroll through spreadsheets. I can't do anything with this blasted cast on."

"You could use VR, Sir."

"I'm not comfortable doing audits in VR," Campbell said. "Doing them on screen is virtual enough. It's hard to hold the reality in your head. I've never been able to really get my head around the numbers in VR."

"Could you remove your cast just for work, perhaps, Sir?"

"No, the doctors told me not to, or the darned thing may never heal properly. And they didn't let me have the controller, either. Knew better, I suppose."

Campbell heaved a huge sigh.

"Commander, could you see if Admiral Childers' launch has lifted yet?"

"Yes, Sir."

Acheson was back in minutes.

"No, Sir. It's still awaiting her return."

"Put a hold on the launch in my name, if you would, then drive me to the shuttle pad."

"Yes, Sir. You going to ask the Admiral's advice?" Acheson asked.

"No, Commander. I'm going up to the ship with her. My work down here is almost done anyhow. Why should I spend the next two weeks down here being frustrated to no end when I can be with her on ship instead?"

CAMPBELL: THE PROBLEM WITH BLISS

"Yes, Sir. Let me get that hold entered."

"Thank you, Commander."

Acheson and Campbell were waiting with the ground car at the shuttle pad when Childers arrived in Admiral Rao's ground car. Campbell's bags were already aboard. The driver let Childers out of the back of Rao's car and she walked up to Campbell.

"What's the matter? Did you forget something?" Childers asked.

"No. I can't work with this thing." Campbell lifted his right arm several inches. "I'm almost done here, anyway. I figured I would just go up to the ship with you."

"You know we are going to be doing maneuvers. Lots of zero-g and high accelerations and flipping ship and all that. Are you sure you're up for it?"

"I'll manage. I'd rather be up there with you than down here being frustrated. With nothing to do, I'll just be waiting around for you to return anyway."

"Well, if you're sure you'll be all right, go ahead," Childers said.

Campbell got on board the launch with the eagerness of a puppy, or a child. Childers just shook her head.

"Thank you, Commander."

"Yes, Ma'am."

Childers boarded the launch as Acheson walked back to the ground cars. The pilot retracted the steps and cycled the hatch. When everyone was clear, he started spinning up the engines.

The launch lifted off the pad smoothly and accelerated into the sky.

On the shuttle pad, Acheson just shook his head.

What a pair, he thought. *It's like she's his mommy.*

On board the launch, Childers laughed.

"Did you see the look on Acheson's face when you scrambled aboard the launch? It was all I could do to keep a straight face," she said.

Campbell laughed along with her.

"Last impressions stick. I wanted to make sure I gave him a good one, so he and the conspirators thought I was truly nothing to worry about. I want them to feel at ease going into the round-up."

"You could have warned me. I've never seen you do the little boy thing before. I almost lost character."

"Even if you had laughed, he would have taken it as the permissive mommy laughing at her little charge. Honest reactions are best. But I am glad to be done with that."

"Me, too," Childers said. "It's so out of character for you, it was like dealing with another person."

"Now you know why theater is a recommended minor in the intelligence track. Some people are good at it, and Intelligence Division wants to train that resource."

"And were you in theater at the Academy?"

"Oh, yes. Wait until you meet Phil Samples."

There were a couple of days yet before *Patryk Mazur* would leave orbit. In his own cabin, down the hall from Childers' on the flag bridge deck, Campbell got ready to go down to Bliss with the last shuttle. It paid to take advantage of being in orbit about a fleet base, and there were maintenance people aboard testing and tweaking and refreshing systems throughout the ship. The last of them would leave just before *Patryk Mazur* left orbit, and Campbell would go down on that shuttle.

The first thing Campbell did when he got aboard *Patryk Mazur* was pull out the controller, connect it to the electrocast, and turn the cast off. It took several minutes to become completely limp again, and he rolled it down his arm and returned it to its pouch. He replaced it in his equipment case. He hated the things – they itched like crazy – but they had their uses.

He put a new, and different-colored, canvas bag on his equipment case so it wouldn't look the same as the one Bill Campbell had been seen with. This one had SAMPLES on the name tape sewn to the bag. He packed a spacer's duffel with Phil Samples' other things, including shipsuits, senior chief petty officer's badges and stripes, identification, civilian clothes, and toiletries. But Bill Campbell's officer uniforms, Intelligence Division, Senior Captain, and Inspector badges, and identification were staying aboard *Patryk Mazur*.

After breakfast Saturday, the day before Campbell was to go down to the surface, he started working on his character. He first shaved off his beard entirely. He used clippers to cut his hair to a half-inch long, then used the clippers without the comb to follow the curve of his forehead up and around the top of his head in a new, balding, hairline. He shaved the top of his head. He then dyed his remaining light brown hair black, after which he added gray at the temples.

He pinched the edges of his eyes vertically to make crow's feet, and used a hypodermic syringe filled with contact cement to make them permanent. Using the same technique, he deepened the creases at the corners of his mouth and center of his brow, and added a slight scar across the jaw line on the left side of his jaw, as if someone had split the skin there with a well-placed punch years ago. He put in dark brown contact lenses to hide his distinctive pale green eyes.

Campbell put on the midnight-blue shipsuit and attached the senior chief petty officer badges and stripes, and the SAMPLES name tape. He assessed himself in the mirror, then touched up one crease at the corner of his left eye. There. That ought to do it.

Childers was in her office, adjacent to and connecting with her cabin, reviewing reports from the ships in her division. When the door buzzer sounded, she pushed the open button on the desk and called out, "Come in."

A senior chief petty officer came in to her office.

"Beggin' your pardon, Admiral, but I'm transferrin' to Bliss tomorrow, and I wanted to tell you how much I enjoyed servin' under you, Ma'am."

Childers was popular below decks, and it wasn't unusual for NCOs transferring out of her command to stop by her office before they left. She rose instinctively to reach out to shake his hand.

"It's been great to have you, Senior Chief Sam–" She stopped dead as she read his name tape, her eyes went wide, and she took in the man before her. "Oh, my God," she said softly.

"Ha! Gotcha!" Campbell said in his normal voice.

Childers sat heavily in her chair. She just stared at him, then started and pushed the button to close the door. As she stared, she began to tick off the changes.

"Looks like you added about ten years," she said.

"Yup. Just coming up on my twenty-four."

"The eyes."

"Have to hide those," Campbell said.

"The hair and beard."

"Which is why I always let them grow out. Quickest disguise in the world is to cut them off. Not that I have much of a beard anyway, but losing it is a big change."

"And the voice," Childers said.

"And the lingo. The below-decks patois. The voice change itself comes with practice. At the Academy, the theater group had us develop an alternative voice with a voice teacher, then practice it by using nothing else for an entire semester. You actually have to work to get your normal voice back, but after that you can switch voice any time you want."

"It's amazing. That'll fool anybody."

"Not quite," Campbell said. "Facial recognition software will give me trouble if someone gets a good shot of me and thinks to run the software. Voiceprint, same thing. And my thumb swipe is the same. Has to be, if I'm going to access my own accounts. And somebody like an Enshin sparring partner would know it was me just by my moves if I tried to spar with him. But it withstands casual scrutiny, which is the requirement."

"Well, it fooled me."

"Which is a good sign. Supper and breakfast brought in to your cabin tonight and tomorrow, so I don't out myself on ship, then I'm off with the last shuttle tomorrow morning."

Return To Bliss

Campbell and Childers were in her office the next morning after breakfast.

"Well, that's it. I'm all packed and good to go," Campbell said.

Childers gave him a hug and a lingering kiss.

"You be careful. I worry about you," she said.

"Oh, and when you're out gallivanting about, playing beamer tag with some Outer Colony fleet, I don't worry?"

"I didn't say that. Be careful."

"I will."

One more quick kiss and he picked up his duffel and the equipment case. Childers went around her desk and pushed the door button, and Campbell was once more Senior Chief Samples, Childers once more Rear Admiral Childers.

"Thanks again, Ma'am, and good spacin' to you."

"Good luck to you, Senior Chief."

Campbell went up-cylinder to the ring corridor and joined the queue for the last shuttle down to Bliss. When he got up to the door, the loadmaster and his assistants were stowing bags. He handed off his duffel to one, then held out the equipment case to another.

"Careful. It's heavy."

"Oof. Boy, I'll say, Senior Chief."

"Maintenance."

"Ah."

Everyone in maintenance built up a set of specialized tools and fixtures they acquired or made over their career, and they carried with them from assignment to assignment. For a senior chief with twenty-three years of service stripes, it was expected to have quite a kit.

Campbell was pointed to a seat and he took it and strapped in. It was a big planetary transfer shuttle. Short-legged, it was meant just for the hop to orbit and back, and that left lots of interior room for passengers and cargo. The shuttles *Patryk Mazur* carried in her normal complement had to have longer ranges, and that crimped the passenger and cargo space a bit.

When the shuttle unlatched from the *Patryk Mazur* and began its descent to Bliss, he had left all of Bill Campbell behind. Only Phil Samples went to Bliss with him.

The shuttle settled down on the pad at Bliss Fleet HQ. Campbell queued to get off the shuttle. By long tradition, deference to his rank among the enlisted didn't extend to transfers between assignments. Everyone queued together.

Outside the shuttle, he queued again for distribution of baggage. As all CSF had name tapes sewed to their duffels and kit, the loadmaster's assistants called names as they pulled bags.

"Samples."

"Here."

After two calls, one for his duffel and one for his equipment case, Campbell headed toward the three buses waiting clear of the pad. One had an "NCO Housing" sign in the windshield, and he got on that one. He put his equipment case on a seat next to the windows, put his duffel on the floor in front of it, and then sat in the seat on the aisle.

The bus was about half full when it was clear all the passengers from the shuttle had boarded buses. The driver got up and faced back down the bus.

"Everybody here bound for NCO Housing? All right, then."

The driver took his seat again and they set off across the base.

At the reception area in the NCO Housing office, there was a line for chiefs and senior chiefs, and two lines for petty officers. Campbell got in the short line for chiefs and senior chiefs. A chief petty officer was serving his line.

"Good morning, Senior Chief."

"Good morning, McCoy."

Chief McCoy read Campbell's name tape and searched his display.

"Samples. Samples. Ah! Here we are. Unit 5-29. That's going to be in Building 5, second to the east heading out the door there. You have your own mess between Buildings 5 and 6, or you can use any enlisted mess on base."

He pushed a thumb-swipe toward Campbell, and Campbell swiped it with his left thumb.

"Right one's all scarred up. Doesn't read."

"Ah. Well, that worked," he said, checking his display. He marked Samples as checked in. "You're all set, Senior Chief."

"Thanks, McCoy."

Campbell walked over to Building 5 and went to unit 29. He swiped his left thumb on the door scanner, and the door unlocked. He went in and looked around. CSF bachelor NCO efficiency apartment, per regulations, one each. It had a tiny kitchenette in the corner, which he might actually need for this assignment, an eating table that looked suspiciously equally suited to playing cards, a comfortable double bed – in case of company, he guessed – a closet, and a bathroom big for his needs, but probably small for a woman's. The CSF's idea of perfect compromise.

Campbell checked the time. Coming up on 12:00. Might as well check out the chief's mess.

After lunch, Campbell walked over to the Planetary Operations Headquarters. He swiped into the building with his left thumb. On assignment to Admiral Rao's office, Phil Samples had access to the building. He went down into the secure basements, where he had given Samples access to Campbell's class 2 secure workspace. He swiped in with the Marine guard using his left thumb.

"That's an old picture," The guard said, checking his display and eyeing him carefully.

"Yeah, they need to fix it, but Personnel keeps makin' excuses. Admiral Rao's secretary said she'd take care of it, so maybe it'll happen now."

The guard nodded and waved him down the hall.

Once in his workspace and logged in as Campbell, he updated the picture in Samples' Personnel file with the picture he took this morning.

Campbell accessed the news feeds for the Joy social calendar. He wanted to see what consulate parties were coming up in the next two weeks.

After that he checked his mail and input/output taps. He found some amusing things there.

> Schenk: On vacation AGAIN?
> Acheson: Yeah, and this time he took his crayons.
> Schenk: Ha, ha.
> Acheson: I'm not kidding.

And this one.

> Schenk: ANOTHER vacation?
> Acheson: No. He broke his arm on vacation, so Admiral
> Mommy took him home to her ship. Gone two weeks.

There was also this exchange off the commercial server, gleaned from the input/output stream. Campbell's software substituted names for the aliases.

> (Schmitt): They don't give morons inspector badges.
> (Schenk): Exception proves the rule. They sure did this time.
> (Schmitt): Perhaps. I don't like it. Keep your heads down.

So John Schmitt was smart enough to worry about him. Campbell would have to play it smart, too. Cat and mouse.

Love 'em or hate 'em, the one thing you can say about a cat is that they are the most patient animals in the world. They can crouch completely still and watch a mouse hole for hours, just waiting for their one opportunity to spring.

Time to go watch the mouse hole.

Campbell had supper in the chief's mess, then changed into civvies and took a bus into town.

He got off the bus at a stop in a poor area not far from the diplomatic district. There were always poor areas in big cities, and cities in the Commonwealth were no different. People fell on hard times, or did not have the capacity or the motivation to escape living on the margins. He looked around, found a slightly more upscale building in the area with rooms to rent by the week, and paid two weeks in advance.

Campbell asked the desk clerk about where he might buy used clothes, and she directed him to a thrift store a couple blocks over. He walked over to the thrift store and picked through their bargain bins to find what he wanted. He bought everything a size or two too large. While he was there, he picked up a canvas bag that had seen better days and a few nicer shirts and pants that fit.

He went back to his room and donned another disguise – a disguise over his disguise. He had brought along some darker shades of makeup from his equipment case. He darkened his skin just a touch, then used the darkest makeup here and there to make himself look dirty. He changed into the more decrepit clothes he had bought, put on a watch cap, and assessed himself in the mirror.

Good enough. Especially at night in the city.

There were refuse cans at intervals along the sidewalk that fronted the big park across the street from consulate row. Campbell worked his way down the line, stopping at cans and rummaging for things that might be sold, or hocked, or still eaten. Once he found the biggest part of a hamburger, only half eaten and still warm. He munched it absently while he rummaged, putting his new-found treasures in the canvas bag.

The cans were of a classic decorative design, spaced vertical slats flaring out at the top, hiding the actual container within. There were two cans near the Duval consulate, one east and one west, both with good views of the front portico of the building, which was accessed by a U-shaped drive off the street. The building wasn't very far back from the public sidewalk, just the width of the drive and a shallow lawn with a sign, "Consulate of Duval." The angle from either refuse can was about thirty degrees off the front wall of the building.

Campbell noted all this while never aiming his head directly at the building. He rummaged in each can in turn as he moved on down the line. Once he was a block from the embassy, he walked into the park and took up a position in the darkness of the edge of some trees and watched the consulate.

After midnight, he meandered across the park and back to his room, where he washed off the make-up and changed back into his original civvies. He walked to the adjacent nightclub area and rode back to the base on one of the special late-night buses for spacers on liberty heading back to Bliss Fleet HQ.

On Monday morning, Campbell walked over to the Planetary

Operations Headquarters. He swiped into the building with his left thumb. The Marine guard checked him against the picture on file, which was the one from yesterday, then nodded and waved him down the hall.

Once in his workspace and logged in as Campbell, he sent a message from the secure account to Captain Ramona Karim, asking her for a meeting in his Class 2 secure workspace at her earliest convenience. He got an immediate message back – "On my way." He marked her as a visitor for this morning on this workspace's access list – which, as the assigned owner, he controlled – so she would be approved by the guard.

It was about ten minutes before there was a knock on the door. Campbell opened the door to find Captain Karim standing there.

"Oh. I'm sorry. This must be the wrong room," Kim said.

"No, you've got the right room, Ma'am. Please come in."

Campbell waved her to one of the guest chairs on the other side of the desk.

"If the Captain would allow, I need to show you somethin'."

Campbell reversed the display so she could see it. He swiped his left thumb, and the terminal brought up the picture and personnel file of Senior Chief Petty Officer Phil Samples.

"Now watch this, Ma'am," Campbell said.

He swiped his right thumb on the pad, and the terminal brought up the picture and personnel file – the front, false personnel file – of Senior Captain Inspector William Campbell.

"That's a cute trick," Karim said.

She sat back and eyed him carefully.

In his own voice, Campbell said, "Sometimes I can't be me and get done what I need to get done, Captain."

"That's a very effective disguise, Sir."

"Thanks. There're only three people who know. Admiral Rao, Admiral Childers, and now you. I couldn't figure out how to accomplish my mission without letting you know. But no one else needs to know, Captain, including your people."

"Can you tell me your mission, Sir?" Karim asked.

"No Sirs. Just Senior Chief. I don't want you to get used to it and say the wrong thing in the wrong place. In broad terms: there is an active espionage ring on this planet, operating within Bliss Fleet HQ, including in Intelligence and Operations. We're going to neutralize it."

"Neutralize it."

"Yes," Campbell said. "We are going to arrest the CSF individuals involved, in a sweep. We are going to do that at a propitious time for our other goals. I'll let you know. I'm still gathering information."

"And I assume there are individuals involved within the diplomatic community?"

"I will take care of any non-CSF individuals. That's not your concern."

Karim nodded.

"What do you need from us?" she asked.

"First, I need you to modify the response to my screamer. Can we add Senior Chief Phil Samples to the protectee list, and distribute his picture?"

"Certainly."

"Can we also get a non-emergency response?" Campbell asked. "An arrest detail response?"

"Yes. The screamer only has one button. Pop the cap and push it. That makes it simple, and not something you have to fumble around with in an emergency. But we can program the response at this end so if you push it once, quick, you get the full armed response. If you push and hold it for two seconds, you get the arrest detail."

"Perfect. Let's do that."

"We'll reprogram it and circulate the new protectee information as soon as I get back to my office."

"All right," Campbell said. "Now let me tell you how this is likely to go down and your role in it."

Red Navy

As *Patryk Mazur* and her division mates spaced out from Bliss, Admiral Childers sent word ahead that Captain Jessen's destroyer division would be joining her heavy cruiser division to form Red Navy for the upcoming exercises. 'Red Navy' was the term applied to the enemy force during CSF exercises, while the defenders were 'Blue Navy.'

Jessen's role got a groan from some of the other division and squadron commanders. The two most devious people in the system – maybe in the CSF – on the same Red Navy? This was going to hurt.

Childers and Jessen devised their attacks while *Patryk Mazur* was in transit to the exercise location, which was outside the inner envelope in case Duval came calling early. Jessen was devious as hell, and Childers found it to be much more of a collaboration than a superior-subordinate relationship. He was particularly good at finding ways to fool the enemy commander into thinking he saw through the surface appearance to what was really going on, only to have what was actually going on be one level deeper still.

They made the exercises the most difficult they could, and the end product was the best set of Red Navy attacks on the Grand Tour yet.

In the end, though, the other divisional and squadron commanders need not have worried. Following the Fleet Book of Maneuvers and having the inside line due to their hyperspace capabilities within the inner and outer system envelopes, Blue Navy was able to outmaneuver the Red Navy attacks in every case. Red Navy was restricted to the published system periphery, and, despite Childers' and Jessen's best efforts, was unable to penetrate Blue Navy's defenses.

At the end of the last exercise, with the crew shouting "We beat Admiral Childers! We beat Admiral Childers!" Vice Admiral Vina Novotny turned to her chief of staff.

"Everybody's celebrating, but they almost got us on that last one. All those restrictions, and they still almost got us," she said.

"Yes, Ma'am, but it was Admiral Childers and Captain Jessen after all."

"I'm just glad they're on our side."

"Amen to that, Ma'am."

The Patience Of A Cat

Every day for the next two weeks, Campbell followed the same routine. He got up late, had a brunch of breakfast steak and eggs in the chief's mess, spent the afternoon in the Planetary Operations Center basement, and then went into town to monitor the Duval consulate until late in the evening.

One night, walking across the park late at night, Campbell was accosted by a pair of young toughs brandishing knives.

"Whaddya want with me, lads? I got nothin' to steal."

"We're not after your money, old man. We're gonna have some fun with ya."

Ah. Sadists. Shit.

Campbell didn't want to kill them, even though that would clearly be a net benefit to society. It could make news, even get stepped-up police patrols in the park, which would make it impossible to achieve his larger goal.

"You don't want to do this, lads. You could get hurt."

They laughed and moved in on him, the leader slashing at him with his knife. Campbell deflected the knife, locked his arm, and took the knife away and tossed it to the side. He used the first fellow as a shield against the second's knife hand until he could get a hold of the other fellow's shirt at the neck. He cracked their heads together hard and they both went down.

Damn. That was harder than just killing them. Well, he had them both down now. What did he do to get them to think twice about their choice of recreational activities, and to leave him alone for the next couple of weeks?

Young fellows. Embarrassment works well on young fellows. What would really embarrass a couple of macho young toughs like this? Hmm. Got it.

Campbell stripped the two young men down, and put their clothes, wallets, knives, shoes – everything – into his canvas bag. He left them lying unconscious, completely naked, in the park.

CAMPBELL: THE PROBLEM WITH BLISS

As an afterthought, he arranged them with one on top of the other and between his legs, as if they were having a go. That ought to do it, no matter which one woke up first.

He wasn't bothered in the park anymore after that night.

There were two consulate parties at other consulates while Campbell had the Duval consulate under surveillance. The driver brought the car up front under the entrance portico fifteen minutes before the party time specified. The consul and his wife, resplendent in their evening wear, came out with John Schmitt and three security men. Two of the security men opened the rear doors on either side of the big ground car for the consul and his wife, while one stood at the door of the consulate and kept an eye on the proceedings. Once the consul and his wife were in the car, John Schmitt got in the front seat on the passenger side, which was the side toward the street.

This was repeated exactly on the second occasion of a consulate party. That was bad tradecraft. They ought to be mixing it up, but it was OK with Campbell if they were sloppy. There was another consulate party next week.

Every afternoon, Campbell pulled up the new information from his taps on the conspirators' mail and input/output streams. There were two interesting developments there.

Ten days or so after they had communicated the plans for the exercises, on the Tuesday of his first week on the planet as Samples, there was an exchange between Schmitt and Singh:

(Schmitt): Any change in status on the upcoming exercises?
(Singh): No. Everything moving ahead per previous plan.

The other thing Campbell noticed is there were no 'keep-alive' messages, no periodic check-ins from the conspirators on base to each other or to Schmitt. Days often went by between messages, and a response might take a day or more, especially on weekends. That was sloppy. It meant the MPs could round up the conspirators within Bliss Fleet HQ at their leisure without Schmitt knowing anything was up.

On Monday of his second week on the planet as Samples, he

received a reply via fast courier mail from Sigurdsen to his original mail about the espionage ring. It was short.

FROM: 22C5654753D58B8EE0591CD60BAE489B
TO: 2C68B1AB7218890C0483C993C600FDF4
SUBJECT: (none)

Round up CSF personnel involved.
Send ppl, evidence to SIG for trial.
For non-CSF, send a message.
Use extreme prejudice.

It wasn't signed, but it didn't need to be. The 128-bit secure terminal designator was his alone, generated when he logged into the secure workspace the first time. The only way to get that designator was to have received a mail from this terminal in the first place. Durand had similarly used a Class 2 secure terminal to send his orders, rather than the Class 3 secure terminal in his office.

Campbell sent a short response in return.

FROM: 2C68B1AB7218890C0483C993C600FDF4
TO: 22C5654753D58B8EE0591CD60BAE489B
SUBJECT: (none)

In process.

Campbell had been going to act anyway, on his general authority and anticipating Durand's likely response. Now he didn't have to act without specific authority. He had it.

After ten days of surveillance, on the Wednesday afternoon of his second week on the planet as Samples, ten days after he had last met with Captain Ramona Karim, he messaged her for another meeting in the Class 2 secure workspace.

"Good afternoon, Captain," Campbell said to her when she arrived.

"Good afternoon, Senior Chief. What is your status? Are we getting close?" Karim asked.

"Yes. We should round up the conspirators in their offices on Friday. We can pick up the two on third shift at their apartments on base. If that goes well, there is a consulate party on Saturday that will be my opportunity to rectify the problem at that end."

"Do we have any part in that last bit?"

"No," Campbell said. "That is not a police matter."

Campbell also asked for a meeting with Admiral Rao in the Class 2 secure workspace that afternoon.

"Good afternoon, Admiral Rao," Campbell said to her when she arrived.

"Good afternoon, Senior Chief Samples. It's good to see you again. I take it this is about that little assignment we discussed a while back."

"Yes, Ma'am. Captain Karim's people are going to round up the entire espionage ring inside the CSF on Friday afternoon. That includes one person in your office."

"Have you gotten all the evidence you need to secure convictions, Senior Chief?"

"Oh, yes," Campbell said. "Caught them red-handed, transmitting the plans for your upcoming exercises to personnel at the Duval consulate, and then confirming just a week ago that those had not changed."

"Excellent. And then what happens?"

"They will be transported to Sigurdsen Fleet HQ for trial and sentencing. That will be your responsibility, Ma'am."

"I can take care of that, Senior Chief," Rao said. "What about the Duval consulate? Will you be taking care of that matter as well?"

"Yes, Ma'am."

"Do you have specific authority there, Senior Chief, or are you acting on general orders?"

"I've received specific authority, Ma'am," Campbell said.

"That's going to get messy, isn't it?"

"Yes, Ma'am."

"Well, be careful, Senior Chief. The lot of them aren't worth one of you."

"I'll try, Ma'am."

Of course, that wasn't the way Intelligence Division thought of it. The message needed to be sent, the way the CSF always sent messages to Outer Colony governments that sought to damage the Commonwealth of Free Planets or its citizens. If CSF personnel were lost in the sending of that message, well, sometimes those things happened.

But, one way or the other, they would get the message.

Extreme Prejudice

On Friday afternoon at 14:00, nine arrest details fanned out across Bliss Fleet HQ from Bliss Military Police Headquarters. Each arrest detail was composed of one officer, usually a lieutenant, and four enlisted men, one of which was at least a petty officer first class.

The MPs overrode the door lock on the apartment of Lieutenant Christopher Sobol, the third-shift supervisor in the Communications Center, and rousted him out of bed.

"Wha'? What's going on?"

"Lieutenant Sobol. You are under arrest. If you would dress, and then come with me, please."

Similarly, the MPs overrode the door lock on Petty Officer First Class Susan Todaro's apartment, the one she shared with Lieutenant Andon Kuang. Todaro, another third-shifter in the Communications Center, was awake, having breakfast.

"Petty Officer Todaro. You are under arrest. If you would come with me, please."

"Shit."

Three arrest details arrived at the Planetary Intelligence Headquarters, and independently headed to different floors within the building.

The first squad of MPs arrested Lieutenant Andon Kuang at his office in the computer section.

The second squad of MPs arrested Commander Veronica Kinley at her office in the counter-intelligence section.

The third squad of MPs arrested Lieutenant Commander Kyle Acheson at his desk outside the office of Senior Captain William Campbell.

Three arrest details arrived at the Housekeeping building, and independently headed to different areas of the building.

The first squad of MPs arrested Petty Officer Third Class Brian Rhee at the furniture inventory counter. He refused to go quietly and had to be subdued.

The second squad of MPs went to Seaman First Class Eduardo Novak's workstation in the security scanning group. Novak wasn't there.

The third squad of MPs arrived at Commander Vilis Schenk's office and let themselves in without knocking.

"Commander Vilis Schenk. You are under arrest. If you would come with me, please, Sir."

Schenk opened his top desk drawer, at which the arresting officer stepped aside and the Seaman First Class behind him brought a machine pistol up onto target.

"Don't even think about it, Sir," the arresting officer said.

At that, Schenk went quietly.

An arrest detail arrived at the Planetary Operations Headquarters and headed directly to the offices of the base commander, Admiral Mary Rao. In the outer office pool, they arrested Lieutenant Mona Singh.

"Lieutenant Mona Singh. You are under arrest. If you would come with me, please."

Admiral Rao came out of her office and watched as Singh was led away. Campbell had not told her who the spy was in her office, lest she somehow let on over the weeks that something was up. That it was Singh shocked her, as the pretty lieutenant had been popular in the office.

The arrestees were held incommunicado from each other and from JAG in the basement detention center of the Military Police Headquarters. Under CSF military justice, with pending espionage charges, they could be held incommunicado for up to a week. They couldn't be questioned without their JAG attorney present, but there was plenty of time for that.

And Campbell didn't need a week.

The failure to apprehend Novak was a problem. By chance, he had been out on a work assignment when the round-up went down, and may have seen the MP vehicles parked in front of Housekeeping when he returned. In any case, he did not return to his workstation that afternoon or to his apartment that evening. The MPs put a bulletin out to all MPs and security personnel at Bliss Fleet HQ to be on the lookout for him, and to apprehend him if seen.

Campbell went into the Planetary Operations Headquarters. Logged into the Class 2 secure terminal in his workspace. He tried to shut down Novak's ability to communicate. He disabled Novak's BCBS account, which Novak could use to contact Schmitt directly, by the simple expedient of blocking login requests to Novak's account at the input/output streams off the base. He also blocked all messages and calls to or from the Duval consulate, and blocked Novak's personal comm. That should block all his means of contact with Schmitt.

The question remained whether Novak had been able to contact Schmitt before Campbell blocked him.

Campbell went into the Planetary Operations Center on Saturday afternoon. He checked his taps on the mail and input/output streams, and found a message from John Schmitt. It was from about an hour before. He logged into BCBS with Schenk's user login name, and sent a reply. Schmitt responded, and Campbell, as Schenk, replied again.

> **(Schmitt): I heard there was some excitement yesterday. You guys OK?**
> **(Schenk): Yeah. MPs busted a drug ring. Nothing to do with us.**
> **(Schmitt): OK, good. Keep your heads down.**
> **(Schenk): Will do.**

There was no other message traffic, and no further replies from Schmitt.

Saturday evening, an hour and fifteen minutes before the official start time of tonight's consulate party, Campbell was fixing a small device to the side of a tree in the park a couple of hundred yards from the Duval consulate. The tree was slightly to one side of a line from the consulate front door to one of the refuse cans along the street.

Forty-five minutes before the official start time of the consulate party, Campbell was working his way down the refuse cans along the street in front of the Duval consulate, as he had every night for two weeks. He got to the can just west of the consulate at about twenty minutes before the party's official start time. He rummaged in the can, and rummaged in his canvas bag.

While rummaging in his canvas bag, he fitted the barrel to the 50-caliber air rifle and spun the B-nut down tight to hold it in place. He chambered one of the special expanding rounds, ensured the safety was off and the gun fully charged from the high-pressure air cylinder. He also turned on the transmitter connected to the trigger. He pretended to rummage in the refuse can again, in the process laying the rifle across the top of the inner can between the decorative staves.

He watched as the car pulled up. When the consul and his wife appeared at the door of the consulate and all eyes were on the local action under the portico, he sank back down behind the barrel as if to rummage in his canvas bag again. He pulled the stock back into his shoulder and lined up the telescopic sight on the scene.

The consul and his wife, dressed in their finest for the night out, got in the car by the rear doors. The two security men closed the doors behind them. They seemed unusually anxious tonight, and scanned the area constantly. Schmitt got in the front passenger seat and reached out to grab the door handle and close the door.

As Schmitt turned to his right to look for the door handle, his eyes scanned across the part of the park in front of him. His gaze locked on Campbell, and Campbell, watching Schmitt's face through the telescopic sight, saw realization come into his eyes, saw him put it all together. Schmitt started to open his mouth to shout a warning. Between breaths, between heartbeats, Campbell squeezed the trigger.

When Campbell pulled the trigger, two things happened. One is that the transmitter sent a signal to the receiver mounted on the tree two hundred yards behind him and slightly to his left. It set off a small firework designed to look and sound like a rifle muzzle flash. It also blew the small device off the tree, and it fell in the grass.

The other thing that happened is the air rifle fired with a small cough. The 50-caliber round left the muzzle subsonic, at about 500 feet per second. It passed between the frame of the windshield and the frame of the car door window, hitting Schmitt, who still had his head turned to his right to look for the door handle, in the left temple.

CAMPBELL: THE PROBLEM WITH BLISS

The round was hollow, scored along the sides, with a fragile nose piece. It blossomed as it plowed through Schmitt's brain, building up a pressure wave in front of it. When it hit the back of his skull, it opened up a three-inch-diameter exit wound along the right lambdoid suture, showering brains, blood, bone fragments, and bits of scalp all over the rear seating area, including the consul and his wife. The bullet continued on to hit the rear window between them, shattering the window and showering them with glass as well.

Campbell let go of the air rifle, and it fell down into the refuse bin. The consul's wife started screaming in shock and horror. The consul security man at the door shouted and pointed toward the muzzle flash he had seen in the park. All three security men pulled semi-automatic pistols out of shoulder holsters and ran down the driveway, across the street and past Campbell.

As the third man ran past him, Campbell pulled a suppressed semi-automatic pistol from the canvas bag. He stood up and shot the running security men in the back, a double-tap to the center of mass for each, beginning with the last one and working his way forward. Each fell down in turn.

Campbell ran to the fallen security men, and double-tapped each of them in the head. He ran back to the refuse bin. Staff were running out of the consulate now to see what was going on.

Campbell took careful aim at the streetlight covering his area, and shot out the light. He retrieved his canvas bag and the air rifle, and disappeared into the darkness.

Undisguised

As he walked across the park, Campbell unscrewed the B-nut and removed the barrel from the air rifle. He dropped both the barrel and the rest of the rifle into the canvas bag with the semi-automatic pistol. He walked back past the dead security men to the tree two hundred yards behind his sniper position, and retrieved his radio device off the lawn.

In the darkness, he pulled an inner plastic bag out of the canvas bag, turned the canvas bag's cleaner inner surface out, and then put the plastic bag back inside it. He changed jackets for one of a different color from the canvas bag, and changed watch caps to one of a different color.

Police sirens were wailing as he walked out of the park and into the poor section west of the diplomatic district. When Campbell got back to his rented room, he washed the make-up off his face and hands, and changed clothes into civvies. He disassembled the weapons and replaced them in the cases carefully, then put those cases in a CSF gym bag, cushioned with towels.

He put the old clothes and anything else that might have his DNA on it, including the bar of soap, into the canvas bag. Then he went around the room spraying everything he touched with a reagent spray to clear his DNA. Toilet handle and seat. Sink faucet handles. Doorknobs. He put the spray in the gym bag at the door and looked around the room for several seconds. Got it.

It was still early as Campbell walked to the bar area. He cut through an alley and dropped the canvas bag in a dumpster behind a restaurant, where it would soon be covered over and soaked through with restaurant garbage.

When he got to the bar area, he got on a base bus that a bunch of spacers on liberty had just gotten out of. He flashed the driver his ID badge.

"Making an early night of it, Senior Chief?"

"Just visitin' relatives. Not much of a bar fly."

"Ah."

CAMPBELL: THE PROBLEM WITH BLISS

Campbell was in bed by 23:00.

On Sunday, Campbell had a large mid-morning breakfast in the chief's mess, then walked over to the Planetary Operations Headquarters. He sent a message to Durand back at Sigurdsen.

FROM: 2C68B1AB7218890C0483C993C600FDF4
TO: 22C5654753D58B8EE0591CD60BAE489B
SUBJECT: (none)

Completed.

He logged into each conspirator account at BCBS, all nine of them, and downloaded the entire account to a memory chip, then wiped the account.

He also saved all his archives, his datasets, his saved views, his notes, and his self-authorizations to access private financial data and personal mail data to the same memory chip. He made two spare copies on additional memory chips.

Campbell also entered orders for Senior Chief Phil Samples to report to Admiral Childers aboard the *Patryk Mazur* when she returned to Bliss orbit.

That done, he erased all his specialized software from the terminal, deleted all the data in this secure account, and closed the secure account with a secure erase request on the user space.

It was almost supper time by the time he completed. He walked over to the chief's mess for supper and made an early night of it.

The next morning, Senior Chief Phil Samples checked out of base housing and took the bus to the shuttle pad for lifts to the *Patryk Mazur*, returning from her exercise drills with the Bliss local defense forces.

"Samples," He said to the load master's assistant as he handed off his duffel.

The load master's assistant checked his list.

"Samples. Got it."

"Careful. This one's heavy."

Campbell handed the canvas bag with the equipment case over.

The assistant load master raised an eyebrow as he took the weight.

"Maintenance," Campbell said, shrugging.

Campbell queued with everyone else and took the seat he was directed to.

The lift to the *Patryk Mazur* was uneventful.

Rear Admiral Jan Childers was reading reports on the just-concluded drills and exercises. With her force restricted to hyperspace transition outside the published system periphery, as an Outer Colony incursion force would be, the Bliss defense forces had handed her division its head in three successive incursion attempts.

That should go a long way to making them understand just how important the training was, and how necessary it was to stick with the standard Fleet Book of Maneuvers.

Childers had a well-deserved reputation as a tactical genius. She was the most decorated officer in the CSF, at any rank. She herself had written the Fleet Book of Maneuvers, while serving on the CSS *Nils Isacsson*. It had been so successful the CSF had made it the standard, imposing it on admirals and captains fleet-wide.

She smiled when she recalled what Vice Admiral Vina Novotny had told her after one particularly devious incursion attempt. "They're over here shouting 'We beat Admiral Childers! We beat Admiral Childers!' I don't think there'll be any more questions or doubts about using the standard book, Admiral Childers."

The door buzzer sounded. Childers pushed the button on her desk to open the door, and a middle-aged senior chief stepped through the door and saluted.

"Senior Chief Samples reporting as ordered, Ma'am."

Childers hit the door button to close the door as she shot up out of her chair. She rounded the desk and threw herself into Campbell's arms.

"Hey, don't knock me down!" he said.

"You're OK! I was so worried," Childers said to his chest.

"Of course, I'm OK."

"Well, there was some pretty lurid stuff in the Joy newsfeeds, and they haven't given the identities of all the bodies yet."

"Yeah, it got a little messy," Campbell said.

"A little!"

"Schmitt, the security coordinator at the consulate, was the ringleader. But it was his security team that beat CSF Commander Michael Chey to death, and Chey was Intelligence Division. We can't let that sort of thing go by without letting them know we don't like it much."

"One against four, with guns?" Childers asked.

"That sounds dicier than it was. I just had to get them looking at that shiny ball over there, then I shot them all from the back. They weren't even facing my direction."

"Nice trick."

"Yeah. It worked," Campbell said, shrugging. "But now, mission is over. The CSF bad guys are all in jail – well, except one, so far – bound for Sigurdsen with the evidence to convict them, the non-CSF bad guys are in the morgue, and the Duval consul to Bliss knows he probably shouldn't have let that sort of thing be run out of his consulate."

"Do you think he knew?"

"If he didn't know, he's incompetent. And Outer Colony governments don't normally post incompetents to their diplomatic missions within the Commonwealth. There are a lot of other Outer Colony worlds they can post those guys to."

"He knew," Childers said, "but you didn't kill the consul."

"No. That would be an escalation. They didn't kill one of our high-ranking diplomatic people. The killed an intelligence officer."

"And so you killed their intelligence officer."

"Yes," Campbell said. "And the men who actually carried out the murder."

"But we lost one guy, and they lost four."

"We lost two guys – Vilis Schenk killed the prior head of Housekeeping, Commander Jukai Clark – plus two destroyers, though not the personnel aboard them."

"Now it sounds unfair the other way," Childers said.

"The world is imperfect. Besides, it isn't all over yet. Schmitt did get the information on the upcoming exercises to Duval. If Duval makes an incursion then, they're going get hurt."

"They're gonna get creamed. But you're done?"

"Yes," Campbell said. "Mission completed."

"And they're not going to retaliate for Saturday?"

"No. The fellow who would normally have carried out that retaliation, and his goons, are all gone. Second, they don't know who actually was the trigger man on Saturday, but they know it wasn't me. I was reported on board the *Patryk Mazur* with a sprained arm."

"So if they did retaliate–?" Childers asked.

"They know the trigger man is still running around somewhere, and that's not good. They might consider retaliating against him, but without knowing who that is, they won't do anything."

"Because he might hit the consul next time."

"Correct," Campbell said. "Also, if they are planning an incursion during the upcoming exercises, they aren't going to want to stir the pot. Rao might cancel the exercises and put the system on alert, and that could go very badly for them when their fleet shows up."

"Then I don't need to wear the body armor on-planet anymore?"

"No. Not on Bliss. Not on this visit, anyway."

"Better and better," Childers said. "Now what?"

"Two weeks on the beach?"

"I like the sound of that. But I do need to visit Admiral Rao first. She asked me to bring you along, actually."

"Well, I have to get out of disguise first," Campbell said. "And we're going to have to borrow her car. I don't have a driver anymore. He's in the clink."

"I'll make it for tomorrow morning."

Back in his own room, Campbell stripped out of his senior chief garb. He got the release agent for the contact cement out of his equipment bag and took out the crow's feet, wrinkles, and scar he had applied. He took out the brown contact lenses. He then shaved his whole head to get rid of the dyed hair and so it could all grow out together.

He put on a shipsuit, and stowed all his Phil Samples gear in his bags. He carefully re-stowed the contact lenses and contact cement release agent in his equipment case.

Campbell then took the air rifle and the semi-automatic pistol out of their cases. He disassembled them and cleaned them to his own exacting standards. These were tools of his trade on which he relied, on which he risked his life, and he took his time. He reassembled them carefully, precisely, lubricating them appropriately as he went.

He polished all his skin oils off the guns and stored them carefully back in their cases, with new desiccant packages from his equipment case. The gun cases went back in the equipment case.

When he finished, it was almost time for dinner. He changed into his uniform to match Childers and went back to her office to pick her up. He buzzed at the door and it slid open.

"Come in," she called.

He walked into her office and the door shut behind him

"Hi, Hon," Campbell said.

"There you are! Where have you been?"

"Oh, around and about."

Childers laughed. It was an easy laugh, with him finally out of danger.

For the time being, anyway.

Duval

On Duval, Rear Admiral Frank Stenberg was once again meeting with his two-up boss, First Space Lord Admiral Carla Scola.

"You're ready to depart, then, Admiral?" Scola asked.

"Yes, Ma'am. We're loaded up and just waiting for some confirmation that the exercises haven't been called off or otherwise changed."

"Do you expect that confirmation to come shortly?"

"Yes, Ma'am," Stenberg said. "Our intelligence asset on Bliss knows our timetable. He'll make an effort to confirm as late as he can and get word to us."

"And Admiral Childers will be gone by then."

"Yes, Ma'am. She's leaving in two weeks, and the exercises are scheduled to begin four weeks from now. So she won't be around. I still have concerns she's built in some kind of trap for us, though."

"But you've changed your strategy for this incursion, haven't you?" Scola asked.

"Yes, Ma'am. If they're prepared for the same thing, we probably have a chance of getting away with this. If not, I'm going to try to get out of there without taking significant losses."

"All right, Admiral. I wanted to talk with you before you left, but it sounds like you have things well in hand. I'll leave you to it, then."

It was later that day that confirmation came in from Bliss.

"That's it, then, Sir," Stenberg's chief of staff, Captain Maryanne Caro, said. "No change in plans."

"I can't believe they're just going to do the same thing again," Stenberg said.

"Well, there is that one quote from their Admiral Rao, Sir. 'What are the odds of such a coincidence occurring twice?' "

"I've got a better question, Maryanne. What are the odds of a moron making line full admiral in the Commonwealth Space Force? Not good, I'll tell you that."

"You think it's a setup, Sir?" Caro asked.

"I wouldn't be at all surprised. Admiral Childers will have spent eight weeks there by the time she leaves. They'll have had to learn something from her. By osmosis if nothing else."

"Yes, Sir. But they can't have anticipated your change in strategy."

"We'll see," Stenberg said. "That's the goal, anyway."

Stenberg sighed.

"All right, Maryanne. Let's give the orders and get underway."

In orbit about Duval, warships ceased spin, folded cylinders, and prepared to get under way.

Four light cruisers, four heavy cruisers, and four destroyers started accelerating toward the system limit and the hyperspace transit to Bliss.

Clean-Up

On Tuesday morning, Bill Campbell and Jan Childers took the Admiral's launch down to the planet. They were met by Admiral Rao's car and driver, and driven to the Planetary Operations Headquarters.

"Go right in, Admiral. Captain. She's expecting you," Lieutenant Commander Rita Allyn said.

"Thank you, Commander," Childers said.

They went into the inner office, where Rao stood to greet them.

"Admiral. Captain. Have a seat, please."

"Thank you, Ma'am," Childers answered for them both.

"I wanted to meet with you both and thank you for your actions here in Bliss, as well as ask you each for a little favor.

"Admiral, I have heard nothing but good reports about the training and exercises you carried out here. At this point, if Duval doesn't attack us during the upcoming exercises, I think people are going to be disappointed. They're starting to call it 'live-fire training.' "

Rao shook her head and Childers laughed.

"I'm glad they're so enthusiastic, Ma'am," Childers said. "From my own point of view, overall the personnel here handled the exercises very well. There are some standouts as well, such as Captain Tien Jessen. He's an amazing talent."

"Yes, and I think he's underutilized, a mistake I'm going to fix."

Jessen's destroyer division had been part of Childers' Red Navy for the last two weeks of exercises, and the man was a devious tactician, a natural talent who had blossomed with the training and exercises.

Along those lines, Admiral," Rao said, "I was hoping you would sit in on our planning session this afternoon. We're hoping to have a little surprise for the Duval forces when they come calling. Captain Jessen will be there as well, along with some other command and tactical personnel. I know you're scheduled for planet leave, but I'm hoping I can delay you just a bit."

"Of course, Ma'am. I'll be happy to help."

"Excellent. Thank you, Admiral.'

Rao turned her attention to Campbell.

"As for you, Captain, I have some news for you. The MPs did pick up Mr. Novak finally. He had gone to ground with some friends on base, and they just kept checking in on known associates until they found him."

"That's good news. So no one slipped away."

"No, we got them all. And I want to thank you for digging into our little problem here and getting it straightened away."

"Thank you, Ma'am. I'm not sure it's all straightened out quite yet, however. This 'incursion,' if you will, – this intelligence failure – shouldn't have gotten this far, and it came close to costing thousands of CSF lives, as well as the lives and infrastructure we're sworn to protect. As it is, it cost us two destroyers and two CSF lives. I suspect there will be some personnel turnover in the command levels of the intelligence operation here before all the dust settles."

"You're right, Captain. Admiral Langford has already been notified his relief is on the way, somewhat early as I understand."

Campbell nodded. No more than he had expected. You didn't investigate who did what to allow that kind of failure to happen before you acted. You replaced the top people immediately and sorted out all the buttons later.

"And there are probably some procedures and methods that will have to be updated in light of the methods they used against us, as well, Ma'am. All that will come out of Sigurdsen eventually, once Intelligence Division headquarters staff has had a chance to look at it all."

Rao nodded.

"I hope so, Captain. But our little mess here is cleaned up, thanks to you and Senior Chief Samples. I'd hoped you would pass on my appreciation to him as well."

Rao said that with a twinkle in her eye.

"Well, I don't know that I'll be seeing him any time soon, Ma'am."

"Oh, I don't know, Captain. He always seems to show up when you need him. When I need him, anyway. That was a particularly nice piece of work he did here, and it has all the rats scurrying back into their holes."

Campbell just nodded. Childers watched the byplay with some humor. It was only a Class 3 secure office, after all.

"And I do have a favor to ask of you, as well, Captain. Captain Karim has asked if you might help her collect the physical evidence, since you know where everything is, or at least have some ideas."

"I'd be happy to help, Ma'am."

"Thank you Captain," Rao said. "With all you two have done already, I probably shouldn't be asking for favors, but I'll not be shy about asking for a little bit more of your time before you go on vacation."

Campbell and Karim and her crew first went to the townhouse. Campbell pointed out the audio bugs one at a time. Karim's crew photographed them in place, then recorded them being removed from the wall by the simple expedient of cutting a six-inch circle of wall board out of the wall. They were bagged as evidence.

Campbell also pointed out the video pickup in the lamp. The entire lamp was bagged as evidence.

The crew went to the next townhouse on either side, then the next, looking for the local re-transmitter. They found it in the third townhouse they checked by using a hand-held radio direction finder. The RDF unit zeroed in on the active transmission that was sending the boosted signals on to another station. It zeroed in on a clock radio in the bedroom of one of the townhouses. The clock radio was bagged as evidence.

Their next stop was Housekeeping. They went through the building looking for the receiver of the clock radio's signal by searching for emissions from the local oscillator. They found the receiver in Vilis Schenk's office.

They searched his office, as well as the furniture inventory area. In Vilis Schenk's office, they found a stash of the small audio bugs and video pickups. In the furniture inventory area, they found two more lamps that had been modified with video pickups.

Everything they found in Housekeeping was bagged as evidence and they moved on to the Planetary Intelligence Headquarters. Once again, in his office and in the Class 2 secure workspace in the basement, Campbell pointed out the audio pickups and they cut out a circle of wall containing them.

CAMPBELL: THE PROBLEM WITH BLISS

Once all those transmitters were removed from the building, they went through the building scanning for more transmitters. Unsurprisingly, they found audio bugs in the office of Senior Captain Bjorn Laterza, the head of counter-intelligence, and in the office of Rear Admiral Sumit Langford, the planetary intelligence commander.

Langford watched them remove the audio bug from his wall with something approaching an expression of disgust on his face. When they showed him the bug from the backside of the wall board, snug in its little hole, he just shook his head.

"Captain Campbell, may I see you for a few minutes?" Langford asked.

Campbell looked at Karim, who nodded.

"That's about it for us, Sir. All we have left to find is the local receiver, and we don't need you for that. Thanks for the help," she said.

"No problem, Captain," Campbell said. Turning to Langford, he said, "Yes, Sir. Here in your office?"

"Now that it's secure, yes, please, Captain."

"Of course, Sir."

Karim and her crew left, closing the door behind them.

"Have a seat, Captain."

Campbell sat in one of the guest chairs facing the desk, and Langford sat down in his desk chair.

"Captain, I owe you both an apology and a thank you. An apology, because after we met six weeks back, I thought you were no more than a Sigurdsen poof. I realize now that was just a disguise. You already knew by that point we had an active espionage ring in operation here, didn't you?"

"I had a strong suspicion, Sir," Campbell said.

"Which is more than I had. That's why I owe you a thank you, Captain. It's one thing to screw up by the numbers, but it's quite another to screw up by the numbers and get a lot of people, both CSF and civilians, killed, and have major loss of infrastructure to enemy action on top of it. That would have been a failure to perform the CSF's prime mission. You saved me from being responsible for that, you and Captain Jessen, and I appreciate it."

"You're welcome, Sir."

Langford nodded.

"It won't save my job, but at least I won't be moved out with that hanging over me. So I have a piece of advice for you, Captain. Just like you, I swore oath to preserve and protect the Charter of the Commonwealth, and this time I was found wanting. This is a young man's game, Captain. I grew too comfortable, too trusting of the people around me, not suspicious enough. It was us against those bad guys out there. I never expected to find the enemy down the hall.

"I should have hung it up a few years back. I have my twenty-four and more, and we have a nice little place on Jablonka, on the coast north of Commonwealth Center. I held on too long, and it could have seriously hurt the Commonwealth. Don't make my mistake, Captain. When it's your time, move on. Let the young people move up. Don't hang on past your time."

It was an incredible admission, and a generous one. Campbell was impressed, despite his earlier dismissal of Langford.

"Thank you, Sir. It's good advice, and I'll try to remember that."

"Good," Langford said.

Langford stood and Campbell followed suit.

"Just so you know, Captain, Admiral Birken has already sent word they are sending my relief out early, which is no more than I would expect. I in turn have passed on my retirement request, with mustering out on Jablonka. Amanda and I will finally be heading home."

"Congratulations, Sir. I hope you enjoy your retirement."

"I'll enjoy it much more than I would have, with nightmares about the dead I let down. Thank you again, Captain."

Campbell and Langford shook hands, and Campbell took his leave.

Langford had screwed up by the numbers, but he owned his mistake. He was an honorable man, and Campbell could respect that.

The tactical planning meeting took place in a Class 1 secure conference room in the basement of the Planetary Operations Headquarters. Attending were Admiral Mary Rao, Vice Admiral Vina Novotny, Rear Admiral Jan Childers, and the squadron and division commanders and tactical officers for all eight divisions of CSF warships stationed on Bliss, including Captain Tien Jessen.

Childers mostly sat and watched. They had all had training in the standard Fleet Book of Maneuvers. They all knew to have the combat elements remain outside of the inner envelope, where they could transition into hyperspace immediately. They all knew the usefulness of destroyers as pickets, and of leaving some of your power hidden in hyperspace.

"One thing we want to do differently this time is keep him coming in, as opposed to last time when Captain Jessen's goal was to get him to balk and leave the system. How do we do that?" Novotny asked.

"One thing to do would be to have the destroyers accelerate toward him at two gravities. That will convince him they really are destroyers."

Childers wasn't sure who said that. It was one of the division tactical officers, she thought.

"We could also have a division or squadron of light cruisers run like crazy for the published system periphery," Jessen said. "Sort of an 'Oh, no, we need to respond right now!' kind of thing."

"And once he gets far enough in, once he's committed, we can have a battleship squadron move into hyperspace and maneuver in behind him," Rao said.

And then Captain Jessen threw the spanner in the works.

"We probably want to have them maneuver around in front of him, because once he sees ships transition to hyper well inside the published system periphery, I would expect he would know he's in trouble, and flip ship. He'll have all his guns pointed out-system to fend off the ships he would expect to come in from behind him. And if our ships come in behind him, they stand a good chance of being booby-trapped by the enemy commander's second force. How do we respond to that second force?" Jessen asked.

There was general hubbub around the table as people commented on his question or tried to ask a question. Admiral Rao claimed the floor by the simple expedient of holding up her hand.

"Please explain, Captain," she said.

"Yes, Ma'am," Jessen said. "Our plans for the exercises are similar to our plans for the previous exercises, and we plan on showing the Duval commander a similar disposition of forces as we did on the earlier incursion. However, as the incursion unfolds, we plan on surprising them. I would expect the Duval commander to similarly show us a similar disposition of forces as on the initial incursion, and to similarly plan on surprising us. The simplest way to do that is with a second force, probably waiting in hyperspace a few light-seconds outside of the published system periphery, where they will be in a position to surprise any of our ships that might try to respond by using hyperspace to get in behind the initial incursion. After the initial incursion force flips ship, our responding ships will be caught between two enemy forces. So I wonder how we will respond to his second force."

Into the stunned silence, Childers said, "That is a brilliant analysis, Captain."

"Thank you, Ma'am," Jessen said. "Oh, and as a side note, we'll know he has a second force along if he brings any destroyers that hold back at the system periphery. Much like your action in Saarestik aboard the *Nils Isacsson*, Admiral Childers."

"You're thinking of the Epsley incursion, where they left a destroyer at the system periphery for signaling to the three heavy cruisers waiting in hyperspace."

"Yes, Ma'am."

Rao looked at Childers. Childers turned to her and gave her a barely perceptible nod.

"All right," Rao said. "It's clear this is one of the more likely possibilities we may face during the upcoming incursion. We will now work out plans for dealing with a potential second force. It seems to me there are two possibilities. First is that the second force transitions out of hyperspace in support of the first force. The second is that the second force transitions out of hyperspace in order to threaten us somewhere else in the system once we have committed our response to the first force. Discussion is open."

"Given that, our response to the first force should probably use only the first division of each of our squadrons, Ma'am, leaving second division to respond elsewhere in the system as required."

That was that division tactical officer again. Commander Pavel Nimsky. Another fellow to keep an eye on.

Departure

Having fulfilled Admiral Rao's favor requests, Bill Campbell and Jan Childers were grabbing a late supper in the Officers Mess between the Planetary Operations Headquarters and the Planetary Intelligence Headquarters.

"So what do you think? We sleep tonight in the townhouse or on ship?" Childers asked.

"On ship? The launch is still here?" Campbell asked.

"Yes. I told them to grab some sleep and hang out a while. They need an hour's warning to saddle up, but we can go up to the ship if you prefer that to the townhouse."

"The townhouse with holes in the walls where they cut the bugs out as evidence? No, thanks."

"The ship, then?" Childers asked.

"I've got a better idea. Why not sleep in the beach house tonight? Can the crew handle that?"

"They should be fresh. Let me ask."

Childers sent a quick comm message, and got a quick response.

"They're actually rested, fed, and ready to go. They said they figured something would be going on after supper."

"Beach."

Intelligence Division would still pick up the tab for the spendy beach resort. Campbell needed to be on Bliss for a while in case there was any retaliation from Duval, but he also needed to be well off base and out of circulation so the potential retaliation couldn't target him. If there was a retaliation, he was the only direct-action operative in position to respond in kind.

After the long day and the two-hour flight, they were dead on their feet by the time they were finally checked in and driven to their beach house.

They woke up in a tangle of arms and legs wrapped in a blanket on the beach. Childers woke first, and just lay quietly in Campbell's arms until he, too, stirred. He looked around in bewilderment at first, completely lost as to where he was. Childers kissed him.

"How the hell did we end up out here?" Campbell finally asked.

"It was your bright idea to go out and sit on the beach before bed, and I think we just fell asleep on the blanket."

"How'd we get rolled up like a burrito?"

"It does get chilly here at night." Childers looked down, then back at him. "Especially when you're lying out on the beach naked. We must have just pulled the blanket around us."

"It's a nice place to wake up, though. I'd give it a ten for style points if nothing else."

"I think the company makes it," Childers said, and kissed him again. This one took longer.

Much longer.

They finally walked hand in hand up the beach to the beach house. They found their uniforms and other clothing in two heaps on the sofa in the living room. They hung everything up, took showers, and started unpacking to find something to wear to breakfast.

"Oh, hell with it. Why get dressed? Let's just order breakfast on the lanai," Campbell said.

"Works for me."

"What a wonderful breakfast," Campbell said with a sigh.

"The food here is top-notch. No doubt about it."

"What's your schedule now? Do you need to go back to the ship before departure?"

"No," Childers said. "All the ships will be on skeleton crews while everybody takes planet leave before the transit to Hutan. I should go aboard a day or two before we leave, but no need until then. Unless something comes up. What about you?"

"Same thing. As long as the comm stays quiet, I'm good until we leave."

"So we've got what? Ten days or so in paradise? I can handle that."

Wednesday morning, Deputy Chief Demyan Tsukuda of the Joy

Police Department, the head of their Homicide Division, stopped by to see Admiral Rao.

"Good morning, Chief," Rao said as they shook hands.

"Good morning, Ma'am. Thank you for agreeing to meet with me."

"No problem, Chief. What can I do for you?"

"Well, Ma'am," Tsukuda said, "you may have heard that we had some excitement in the diplomatic district in Joy last Saturday."

"Yes. A quadruple murder. Shocking."

"Yes, Ma'am. The security coordinator of the Duval consulate and three members of his security team. It occurs to us that there may be some connection between those murders and the CSF base here on Bliss."

"How so, Chief?" Rao asked.

"Well, Ma'am, maybe a month back, Senior Captain William Campbell came to see me. He was asking about the murder of a CSF officer, Commander Michael Chey, in the diplomatic district, after attending a party at the Duval consulate. I was wondering if this latest incident might be some sort of payback for Commander Chey."

Rao typed at her terminal for a few seconds, and looked back up at Tsukuda.

"Our records show Captain Campbell as off-planet, on a ship in orbit, for eighteen days, returning to the base here yesterday morning. I met with him myself yesterday."

"Oh, I wouldn't suspect Captain Campbell, Ma'am. As I say, I've met him. I was wondering if it were someone else, acting on his information."

"I can assure you, Chief," Rao said, "no one under my command had any orders to carry out any sort of payback or anything of the sort that could have resulted in Saturday night's events. Now, whether it was some sort of love triangle gone bad or something, I couldn't say. But Saturday night's murders weren't committed under my authority."

"Ah. Well, that's that, then. And I doubt a love triangle would result in four murders of this sort. I've watched the security tapes and the whole thing took under a minute and ended with two shots to the head of each of the members of the security team. That looks like a professional hit to me."

Tsukuda sighed.

"These sorts of things are always very difficult. Political murders are always a mess. We have over a hundred foreign consulates in Joy, one from Earth, of course, plus most of the Outer Colonies. And they're always playing cat and mouse with each other."

"Wow. All in all, I think I'd rather have my job than yours, Chief."

"Yes. Well, thank you for your time, Ma'am. I didn't hold much hope for an answer here, but one does need to cover the bases."

"Understood, Chief. And if there's anything else I can do to help, don't hesitate to get in touch."

Tsukuda left and Rao thought back over the conversation. She hadn't lied to Tsukuda. Not exactly. Senior Captain William Campbell reported directly to Sigurdsen, and was not under her command authority. And their records did show him aboard CSS *Patryk Mazur* for those eighteen days.

On Saturday morning, after ten days at the resort, Campbell and Childers were waiting on the shuttle pad after another one of those terrific breakfasts, watching the admiral's launch from the *Patryk Mazur* maneuver for a landing.

They had solved their unpacking problem by the simple expedient of sending all their clothes, including their uniforms, out for laundering, and spent the ten days not wearing anything at all. As a result, being back in uniform seemed strange to the point of alien, though they both looked splendid in their professionally laundered and pressed uniforms. In this, as in everything else, the resort exceeded every expectation.

As the shuttle lifted into the air, they watched the resort fall away below them. First the central buildings, then the widely scattered beach houses along the miles of beach.

"Well, now we know why they call it Bliss," Childers said.

The admiral's launch took them directly to the *Patryk Mazur* in orbit. They had said their goodbyes to Admiral Rao last Tuesday.

The shuttle docked in its own bay on the bow, outboard of the main shuttle bays. Other shuttle operations were held while the admiral's launch docked and the bow wall rotated up to speed to match the ship before the ship's docking tube was extended to the launch. The more outboard location gave a slightly higher apparent gravity than docking closer to the rotational center of the ship.

Admiral Childers' aide was standing by with a baggage crew to take their things to their cabin, so Campbell and Childers debarked the shuttle and headed directly to their quarters.

The flat, slightly stale smell of recycled shipboard air was both a shock and a welcome home after so long at the tropical resort.

Childers was on the flag bridge Monday morning when the squadron was ready to break orbit.

"All ships report ready for departure, Ma'am."

"Squadron orders. Prepare to make way."

"Yes, Ma'am. Squadron orders, prepare to make way, transmitted."

The maneuvering warning sounded, and the *Patryk Mazur* started slowing its spin until it finally hung stopped in its orbit. There was zero gravity aboard the ship. There was a slight lurch and feeling of movement as the crew cylinders folded back against the ship. A distant metallic clatter and clanking marked the cylinders being latched in place.

"All ships report ready to make way, Ma'am."

"Squadron orders. Space for zero mark zero-nine-zero on the planet, one gravity acceleration."

"Yes, Ma'am. Zero mark zero-nine-zero on the planet, one gravity. Spacing orders transmitted."

Apparent gravity gradually built until there was a full one-g on the flag bridge. Under rotation, so high in the cylinder, it had been only 0.4 g in orbit.

"All ships report under way, Ma'am."

Childers watched Bliss fall away behind them in the display. She wondered how they would fare against the Duval incursion if it came.

Second Incursion

Rear Admiral Frank Stenberg of the Duval Space Navy was still flying his flag on the light cruiser DNS *Solar Wind*. The light cruisers would be the first to make hyperspace transition into the Bliss system, and he wanted to be in a position to evaluate what was going on and make command decisions in normal-space, not sitting in hyperspace.

He hoped he had a tactical plan that would work against the likely CSF reaction to his incursion attempt. Unlike some other DSN officers, he had a healthy respect for the CSF, and he knew they would have made accommodations to counter him after his last incursion attempt. He also worried about Admiral Childers and her squadron having just been here for training and exercises. He had planned and gamed his moves to several likely scenarios.

He just hoped they were good enough.

Aboard DNS Solar Wind

The division of Duval light cruisers, with two destroyers riding shotgun, transitioned out of hyperspace right on the system periphery of Bliss at zero mark ninety on Bliss-6.

"Hyperspace transition complete," Duval Space Navy Lieutenant Henry Ambrogi said.

"We're collecting data now, Sir," Lieutenant Commander Debra Hansen said. "We have multiple warships – at least two squadrons, probably three – active around Bliss. Hard to make it all out at this distance."

"And Bliss-6?" asked Stenberg.

"We have eight ships at standby power levels in orbit around Bliss-6, Sir. No class determination possible yet."

"Keep an eye on them, Commander. Let me know as soon as they power up."

"Yes, Sir."

"Let's get under way, Mr. Ambrogi. Division orders. Set course for Bliss-6c at 1.7 gravities."

The four light cruisers got under way, while the destroyers

remained at the system periphery.

Aboard CSS Whittier

"Sir, we have a hyperspace transition at zero mark zero-nine-zero on Bliss-6," Lieutenant Theresa Sato said. "Right on the system periphery. Six warships, Outer Colony design. I make them as four light cruisers, two destroyers. The cruisers are beginning acceleration toward Bliss-6 at 1.7 gravities."

"Squadron orders," Jessen said. "Power up and set course zero mark zero-nine-zero on Bliss-6 at two gravities."

"Set course zero mark zero-nine-zero on Bliss-6 at two gravities. Orders transmitted, Sir."

Aboard CSS Hannibal

"Ma'am, we have a hyperspace transition at zero mark zero-nine-zero on Bliss-6. From this distance it's hard to tell much, but it looks like four light cruisers and two destroyers. Outer Colony design. The cruisers are beginning acceleration toward Bliss-6," Lieutenant Anish Krueger said.

"The destroyers are staying put?" Admiral Vina Novotny asked.

"Yes, Ma'am. They are stationary at the system periphery."

"Right on profile, George. And they brought destroyers this time," Novotny said to her chief of staff.

"Do you think Captain Jessen is right, Ma'am? That means they have another force sitting in hyperspace?" Senior Captain George Kang asked.

"No other reason for it. They're standing picket. Let's go ahead and get Admiral Kohut on his way."

"Yes, Ma'am."

Aboard CSS Siberia

"Sir, message from Admiral Novotny. Spacing Plan Orange-2."

"All right. Squadron orders. Orange-2. Maximum acceleration," Rear Admiral Andro Kohut said.

The Orange group of maneuvers were specials. Not in the Fleet Book of Maneuvers, they were drawn up special for this potential incursion. Orange-2 was 'head to the nearest system periphery as fast as you can.'

The idea was to convince the Duval incursion to keep coming in, deeper into the system, and trap them there.

Aboard DNS Solar Wind

"They've powered up, Sir," Hansen said. "I make it eight destroyers. Coming out to meet us at two gravities."

"Two gravities?" Stenberg asked.

"Yes, Sir. Two gravities."

Stenberg's chief of staff, Captain Maryanne Caro, came up alongside him. "Well, Sir, they must have replaced the two destroyers they lost, because this time they're definitely all destroyers."

"And they're not afraid to let us know it, which does not give me a good feeling. Let's keep our eyes open for the other shoe to drop."

"Yes, Sir."

"Sir," Hansen said. "I just picked up a squadron of light cruisers making for the system periphery from that gaggle of ships around Bliss. They're pulling 1.75 gravities, Sir."

"They're pushing their margins awfully hard to do that, Sir," Caro said.

"Yeah, that sure looks like a knee-jerk emergency response to me. So maybe we really did catch them by surprise."

Aboard CSS Hannibal

Travel in from the published system periphery was measured in days, even at 1.7 or 2 gravities. The tension on all the ships involved grew as the hours passed.

Finally, eight hours after the incursion began, Admiral Novotny gave the order.

"Fleet orders. Orange-4. Division orders. Red-5 at ten light-seconds from the system periphery."

Hiding on the other side of the sun from Stenberg's ships, Admiral Novotny's CSS *Hannibal*, and her division mates, the CSS *Akbar*, the CSS *Ulysses S. Grant*, and the CSS *Scipio Africanus*, slipped into hyperspace unnoticed.

Aboard CSS Anderson Lail

"Fleet orders, Sir. Orange-4."

"All right. Division orders. Red-5 on the system periphery at zero mark zero-nine-zero on Bliss-6. Maintain hyperspace generators on standby," Rear Admiral Salvatore Heyerdahl said, aboard his flagship, the heavy cruiser CSS *Anderson Lail*.

In naming their heavy cruisers, the CSF had run out of signers of the Charter of the Commonwealth, so they had moved on to other heroes of the War of Independence.

The CSS *Anderson Lail* and her division mates, the CSS *Marc Heller*, the CSS *Jennifer Lowenthal*, and the CSS *Brian Holcomb*, disappeared into hyperspace.

Aboard DNS Solar Wind

"Sir, I just had a division of CSF heavy cruisers disappear into hyperspace," Hansen said.

"How did they get to the system periphery?" Stenberg asked.

"They didn't, Sir. They transitioned from where they were. About twenty-five percent of the way in from the periphery."

"There's the other shoe dropping, Maryanne," Stenberg said to his chief of staff.

"If they can transition inside the system periphery, we've got troubles," Caro said.

"Maybe, maybe not. The approaches to Bliss have to be the most well-mapped in the whole system. I doubt they can pull that off just anywhere. Still, I think we should flip ship and get headed out of here, at least for the moment."

"Yes, Sir."

"Division orders. Flip ship and resume acceleration."

"Division orders transmitted, Sir."

Stenberg's division continued on toward Bliss-6, even as its acceleration toward the system periphery began reducing their velocity. It would be eight hours before they came to a halt, and another eleven hours before they passed the system periphery on the way out.

Meanwhile, the division of CSF destroyers continued to close the distance. At this rate, they would catch Stenberg's light cruisers before they would pass beyond the system periphery.

Hours passed without any sign of the CSF heavy cruisers. Stenberg's division finally slowed to a halt and started building velocity out of the system.

After eight more hours accelerating toward the system periphery, with the CSF destroyers now only twelve light-seconds behind them, they were halfway out from where they had come to a stop. Since they weren't going to decelerate, but keep right on accelerating, they had only three more hours until they could escape the system.

Aboard CSS Whittier

"Distance to enemy cruisers?" Jessen asked.

"Twelve light-seconds, Sir."

"Have we passed into the outer system envelope?"

"Yes, Sir. We just passed the boundary."

"Squadron orders. Hyperspace transition on the mark. Communications, stand by to transmit tactical plot. Five... Four... Three... Two... One... Mark."

The CSS *Whittier* and her seven squadron mates executed a synchronized transition into hyperspace. With transition complete, *Whittier* transmitted the tactical plot to Admiral Heyerdahl aboard the *Anderson Lail*.

Aboard DNS Solar Wind

"Sir, those destroyers just hypered out," Hansen said.

"OK, here's where it gets interesting. Keep an eye on the system periphery. Tell Captain Donati aboard *Swift Spear* to stand by."

"Yes, Sir."

Aboard CSS Anderson Lail

"Sir, we have the tactical plot from the *Whittier*."

Heyerdahl looked at the plot with a critical eye. All was proceeding as Orange-4 had anticipated. No reason to diverge from the plan now.

"Division orders. Hyperspace transition on the mark, maintain hyperspace generators on standby, and prepare for immediate transition back into hyperspace."

"Division orders transmitted, Sir. Counting down."

Aboard DNS Solar Wind

"Sir, hyperspace transition dead ahead. Four heavy cruisers at the system periphery."

"Order Captain Donati to execute Paul Revere," Stenberg said.

"Aye, Sir."

The two destroyers had been accelerating away from the system periphery, and the four CSF heavy cruisers had transitioned into normal-space right on top of where they had been. The destroyers transitioned into hyperspace.

Aboard CSS Anderson Lail

"Sir, those two destroyers just transitioned into hyperspace."

"Division orders," Heyerdahl said. "Red-4 on the enemy cruisers at six light-seconds. Firing Plan Alpha. Guns free. Transmit tactical plot to *Hannibal* on transition."

The *Anderson Lail* and her cohorts disappeared into hyperspace.

"Hyperspace transition complete. Transmitting tactical plot to *Hannibal*."

Aboard DNS Galactic Rim

"Sir, the *Swift Spear* has transitioned. Captain Donati has transmitted the tactical plot."

Aboard the heavy cruiser DNS *Galactic Rim*, Rear Admiral Robert Siegel had been waiting in hyperspace for hours for this moment.

"Division orders. Hyperspace transition. Guns free. Fire at will."

"Orders transmitted, Sir."

Aboard CSS Hannibal

The CSS *Hannibal* and her division mates had spent the intervening sixteen hours in hyperspace, circumnavigating the inner boundary of the inner envelope – the hard system limit – from hiding behind the sun on the other side of the system to ten-light seconds outside the point on the published system periphery where the hostile incursion had first appeared. Admiral Novotny had been in position for only a little over an hour when the tactical plot came in from the *Anderson Lail*.

"Division orders. Hyperspace transition on the mark. Firing Plan Alpha. Guns free," Novotny said.

"Orders transmitted, Ma'am. Counting down."

After Captain Jessen's destroyers disappeared into hyperspace, everything happened very quickly.

The heavy cruisers CSS *Anderson Lail*, CSS *Marc Heller*, CSS *Jennifer Lowenthal*, and CSS *Brian Holcomb* appeared at the system periphery.

The destroyers DNS *Swift Spear* and DNS *Swift Arrow* disappeared into hyperspace.

The heavy cruisers CSS *Anderson Lail*, CSS *Marc Heller*, CSS *Jennifer Lowenthal*, and CSS *Brian Holcomb* disappeared back into hyperspace.

The heavy cruisers DNS *Galactic Rim*, DNS *Galactic Center*, DNS *Galactic Arm*, and DNS *Galactic Drift*, together with the destroyers DNS *Swift Spear*, DNS *Swift Arrow*, DNS *Swift Spur*, and DNS *Swift Foot*, appeared three light-seconds outside of the system periphery, ready to fire on Admiral Heyerdahl's heavy cruisers, only to find they were no longer there.

The heavy cruisers CSS *Anderson Lail*, CSS *Marc Heller*, CSS *Jennifer Lowenthal*, and CSS *Brian Holcomb* appeared directly in front of Admiral Stenberg's division of light cruisers at six light-seconds, outside of his range of them, but within their range of him.

The battleships CSS *Hannibal*, CSS *Akbar*, CSS *Ulysses S. Grant*, and CSS *Scipio Africanus* appeared ten light-seconds outside the published system periphery and seven light-seconds behind Admiral Siegel's heavy cruisers and destroyers, which had all their guns pointed in the other direction.

The outcome of heavy cruisers firing on light cruisers or battleships firing on heavy cruisers is seldom in doubt. The heavier ship's beams can strike the lighter ship from outside its range, cutting through its shields like they weren't there.

The Commonwealth Space Force ships opened fire immediately on returning to normal space, and all the Duval Space Navy ships in the Bliss system disappeared into fireballs and clouds of debris under their withering fire.

Hutan

"Squadron orders. Prepare for hyperspace transition," Rear Admiral Jan Childers said on the flag bridge of the *Patryk Mazur*.

"Yes, Ma'am. Prepare for hyperspace transition. Orders transmitted."

They were approaching Hutan after a three-week crossing. Stop number six on the Grand Tour of eight planets in two years.

"All ships report ready for transition, Ma'am."

"Squadron orders. Hyperspace transition on the mark."

"Yes, Ma'am. Squadron orders, transition on the mark. Five... four... three... two... one. Mark."

Childers felt her stomach wiggle for a split-second, and then the display came alive with the normal-space view.

"All ships report transition complete, Ma'am."

"Mr. Krueger, anything special going on?" Childers asked.

"No, Ma'am. System scans are normal status. No foreign military vessels present. CSF and commercial traffic patterns normal," Lieutenant Krueger said.

"Thank you, Mr. Krueger. Squadron orders. Prepare to make way. Course –"

"Three-three-five minus zero-one-five on the sun, Ma'am," Krueger said.

"Three-three-five minus zero-one-five on the sun, at one gravity."

"Yes, Ma'am. Squadron orders, three-three-five minus zero-one-five on the sun, at one gravity. Orders transmitted."

It was still several days to Hutan from the published system periphery, which Commonwealth ships were scrupulous to use in non-combat and non-emergency situations. No sense letting every foreign-flag commercial ship in the system report back to their planet what the Commonwealth's capabilities were.

"All ships report prepared to make way, Ma'am."

"Squadron orders. Space on the mark."

"Yes, Ma'am. Space on the mark. Five... four... three... two... one. Mark."

Apparent gravity on the flag bridge gradually came back up to one gravity as the ship's engines were throttled up.

"All ships report under way at one gravity, Ma'am."

The alarm system sounded the soft ding-ding of standing down from maneuvering and hyperspace transition.

Campbell and Childers were in her ready room reviewing the mail they had picked up on coming into the Hutan system.

"Oh, my," Childers said. "I got an AAR from Admiral Rao. Duval did attempt another incursion."

"What happened?"

"CSF cleaned their clocks. And Jessen was right. There was a second force. Four heavy cruisers lurking in hyper as back-up."

"Wow," Campbell said.

"Yeah, but the signaling destroyers were a clue to their presence, as Jessen had warned, and Admiral Novotny waylaid them. Duval's total losses were a division each of heavy cruisers, light cruisers, and destroyers."

"What about CSF losses?"

"Minor shield damage," Childers said. "No losses of ships or personnel."

"Well, that'll teach 'em."

"And in the mail with the AAR, Admiral Rao says she put in for promotion to Senior Captain for Tien Jessen. She wants to put him on Novotny's tactical team."

"Smart move," Campbell said."

"Yeah." Childers scanned down the rest of her mail. "That's the big stuff. What about you."

"I got a note from Admiral Birken."

"Birken, not Durand?" Childers asked. Admiral Birken was the head of the Intelligence Division.

"Yep."

"Wow. What's it say?"

" 'Nice job.' "

"Nice job?" Childers asked. "That's it? No medals or promotion or anything?"

"That's not how Intelligence Division works. Medals or a promotion would be a public acknowledgement something happened, and I was involved. That would not be good."

"I can't believe you put your life on the line and dig out a major espionage ring and, and do that other stuff, the messy stuff, and you get nothing."

"A personal note from Admiral Birken, saying 'Nice job?' That's not nothing. That's everything. That's as good as it gets. And there's one more thing."

"What's that?"

"Intelligence Division never forgets."

Appendix

Inhabited systems mentioned (capital city)

Earth (New York City)

Members of the Commonwealth of Free Planets:

Anders
Bahay (Kabisera)
Bliss (Joy)
Boomgaard
Calumet
Courtney
Hutan
Jablonka (Jezgra)
Kodu
Meili

Mountainhome
Natchez
Pahaadon
Parchman
Saarestik
Shaanti
The Yards [Doma]
Valore
Waldheim

Outer Colonies

Alpen
Arramond
Becker
Brunswick
Coronet (Jewel)
Drake
Duval
Epsley
Feirm
Ferrano
Grocny
Guernsey
Lautada
Melody

Mon Mari
New Carolina
Nymph
Oerwoud
Paradiso (Corazon)
Refugio
Samara
Seacrest
Stadt (Dorf)
Svobodo
Tenerife
Villam
Wolsey

Notes on Navigational Notation

The Commonwealth Space Force uses the following standards with respect to navigational bearings and distances.

Navigational bearing and distance are specified as:

rotation mark/minus elevation (on point) (at distance)

All such references are with respect to a point, a baseline, and a plane.

- If no point is specified, the point is the ship, the baseline is the long axis of the ship projected through the bows, and the plane is defined by the plane of the ship with the command cylinder(s) considered to be 'up'.

- If another ship is specified as the point, such as 'on the enemy', the point is the enemy ship, the baseline is the vector of the enemy ship's velocity, and the plane is the plane of the ecliptic.

- If a planet is specified as the point, the point is the planet, the baseline is a line from the planet to the sun, and the plane is the plane of the ecliptic.

- If a sun is specified as the point, the point is the sun, the baseline is a line from the sun to the primary inhabited planet, and the plane is the ecliptic.

- If the galactic center is specified as the point, the point is the galactic center, the line is the line from the galactic center to the ship, and the plane is the plane of the galactic lens.

Bearing angles are always specified as 'number-number-number'. Designations such as 'ninety-three' and 'one-eighty' are not permitted. These are correctly specified as 'zero-nine-three' and 'one-eight-zero'.

An exception occurs for 'zero-zero-zero', which may be stated simply as 'zero', such as in 'zero mark zero' or 'zero mark one-eight-zero'.

rotation is specified as 'number-number-number' in degrees clockwise from the projection of the baseline onto the plane when viewed from above. Leading zeroes are included, not dropped. number-number-number runs from zero-zero-zero to three-six-zero.

- If the point is the ship, 'above' means from above the ship with the command cylinder(s) considered to be 'up'.

- If the point is an enemy ship, a planet, or the sun, 'above' means from the north side of the solar system as determined by the right-hand rule: with the fingers of the right hand in the direction of orbit of the planets, the thumb points north.

- If the point is the galactic center, 'above' means from the north side of the galaxy, as determined by the right hand rule applied to the rotation of the stars about the galactic center.

elevation is specified as 'mark/minus number-number-number' in degrees up/down from the plane. 'mark' is used for bearings above the plane, and 'minus' is used for bearings below the plane. 'Above' is defined as for rotation. Leading zeroes are included, not dropped. number-number-number runs from zero-zero-zero to one-eight-zero.

distance is specified in light-units, most frequently in light-seconds.

CSF ships mentioned, by class
First ship in class is underlined

Battleships (BB)
CSS Amazon
CSS Artemisia
CSS Boadicea
CSS Cleopatra
CSS Jean d'Arc
CSS Kriegsmädchen
CSS Lakshmibai
CSS Tomoe
CSS Zenobia

CSS Akbar
CSS Alexander
CSS Belisarius
CSS Genghis Khan
CSS Georgy Zhukov
CSS Hannibal
CSS Julius Caesar
CSS Marlborough
CSS Napoleon Bonaparte
CSS Scipio Africanus
CSS Sun Tzu
CSS Ulysses S. Grant
CSS Zheng He

Heavy Cruisers (BC)
CSS Aluna Kamau
CSS Anderson Lail
CSS Donal McNee
CSS Gerald Ansen
CSS Guadalupe Rivera
CSS Hu Mingli
CSS Ikaika Kalani
CSS Jane Paxton
CSS Jacques Cotillard
CSS Manfred Koch

CSS Matheus Oliveira
CSS Mineko Kusunoki
CSS Nils Isacsson
CSS Patryk Mazur
CSS Roman Chrzanowski
CSS Sania Mehta
CSS Willard Dempsey

Light Cruisers (CC)
CSS Aquitaine
CSS Caribbean
CSS Catalonia
CSS Great Plains
CSS Gujarat
CSS Kansai
CSS Midwest
CSS Provence
CSS Schwarzwald
CSS Siberia
CSS Sichuan
CSS Tuscany

Destroyers (DD)
CSS Bennington
CSS Brenau
CSS Clermont (DD-ST)
CSS Elmhurst
CSS Emery
CSS Hamilton
CSS Howard
CSS Knox
CSS Maryville
CSS Middlebury
CSS Pomona
CSS Whittier

CSF ship capabilities, by class

Battleships (BB)

Classes: *Cleopatra*, *Alexander*
Crew Complement: 2400
Maximum Acceleration: 1.1 gravities
Guns, number: 6
Guns, type: 'battleship-grade', 'super-heavy'
Guns, range: 10 light-seconds

Heavy Cruisers (BC)

Classes: *Gerald Ansen*
Crew Complement: 1200
Maximum Acceleration: 1.4 gravities
Guns, number: 3
Guns, type: 'heavy'
Guns, range: 7 light-seconds

Light Cruisers (CC)

Classes: *Tuscany*
Crew Complement: 800
Maximum Acceleration: 1.7 gravities
Guns, number: 3
Guns, type: 'medium'
Guns, range: 5 light-seconds

Destroyers (DD)

Crew Complement: 400
Maximum Acceleration: 2.1 gravities
Guns, number: 3
Guns, type: 'light'
Guns, range: 3 light-seconds

Major Awards and Decorations to Jan Childers

The Commonwealth Charter Medallion
Battle of Kodu
CSF Combat Medal, with three clusters
Battle of Parchman
Battle of Feirm
Battle of Kodu
Battle of Earth
CSF Science Medal, with cluster
Calculation of the system periphery; hyperspace modulation
Calculation of the inner and outer system envelopes
Distinguished Service Medal, with three clusters
Battle of Valore
Battle of Saarestik
Battle of Calumet
Battle of Feirm
Victorious Action ribbon, with one gold and one silver star
Battle of Valore
Battle of Parchman
Battle of Saarestik
Battle of Pahaadon
Battle of Feirm
Battle of Kodu
Battle of Earth
Theater of Service Ribbons

Valore	Natchez
Parchman	Meili
Saarestik	Bliss
Pahaadon	Hutan
Calumet	Mountainhome
Bahay	Shaanti
Waldheim (with star)	Kodu
Courtney	Jablonka

The Earth Medal

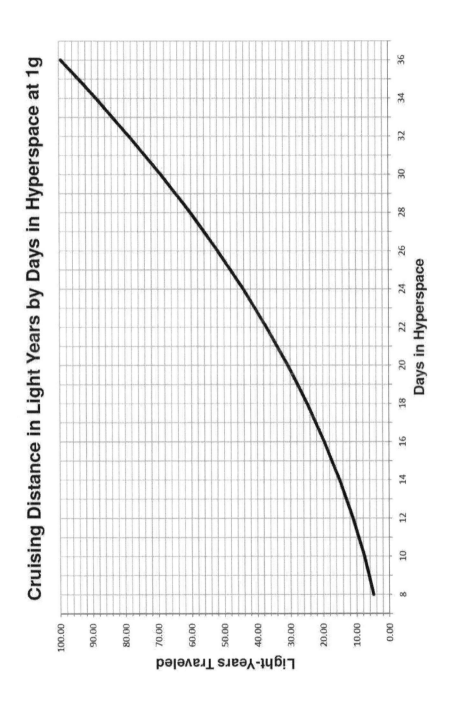

RICHARD F. WEYAND

Acronyms and Terms

AAR – After Action Report.
AO – Area of operations.
ATO – Assistant Tactical Officer.
ATS – Advanced Tactics School.
below decks – cylinders on a ship containing enlisted quarters and mechanical areas such as propulsion, weapons control, etc.
blue team – defender in a war game exercise.
BMS – Brunswick Merchant Ship.
bogey – an unidentified contact, such as on radar.
BSF – Becker Space Force.
BSN – Brunswick Space Navy.
BTS – Basic Tactics School.
building book – designing a book of maneuvers.
bulkhead – wall on a spaceship.
CCM – CSF decoration, Commonwealth Charter Medallion.
CCS – ship prefix, Commonwealth Colony Ship.
CFP – Commonwealth of Free Planets.
CIC – Combat Information Center.
Class 1 secured facility – the highest rated facility for the use or discussion of classified materials.
CM – CSF decoration, Combat Medal.
CNO – Chief of Naval Operations.
Commonwealth – Commonwealth of Free Planets.
CPS – ship prefix, Commonwealth Passenger Ship.
CSF – Commonwealth Space Force.
CSL – Commonwealth Star Lines, commercial passenger company.
CSS – ship prefix, Commonwealth Space Ship.
deadhead – make a trip aboard ship while not serving; guest; ferry.
deck – floor in a spaceship.
deckhead – ceiling in a spaceship, with a room directly above.
division – half of a squadron; in CSF, four ships.
DNA – deoxyribonucleic acid; a molecule of genetic instructions.
door – physical closure on a doorway; may not be airtight.

166

doorway – opening in a bulkhead.

DSM – CSF decoration, Distinguished Service Medal.

DSN – ship prefix, Duval Space Navy.

ENS – ship prefix, Earth Navy Ship.

Enshin – martial art combining karate and judo, founded in 1988.

Exam – Citizenship Exam of the Commonwealth of Free Planets.

Fleet Book (of Maneuvers) – CSF standard book of maneuvers.

flotilla – two squadrons under one command; usually destroyers.

g – one gravity, the amount of gravity one feels on Earth.

GMD – Galactic Mail And Defense Corporation.

geosynchronous – west-to-east orbit in 24 hours; geostationary.

Goat Locker – Chief's Mess on a ship.

hatch – airtight cover on a hatchway in a deckhead or overhead.

hatchway – opening in a deckhead or overhead, with a hatch.

HQ – Headquarters.

inner envelope – calculated volume inside the published system periphery allowing hyperspace cruise but not transition.

IS – interstellar.

JAG – Judge Advocate General, the legal arm of the CSF.

JTO – Junior Tactical Officer.

ladderway – opening in a deckhead or overhead, without a hatch.

light-second – distance light travels in one second; 186,282 miles.

light-year – distance light travels in one year; 5.88 trillion miles.

low-g – low gravity; gravity under 0.2 g.

metroplex – city and its suburbs; metropolitan area.

LNS – ship prefix, Lautadan Navy Ship.

MP – Military Police.

NOC – Naval Operations Center at Sigurdsen Fleet HQ.

OCS – Officer Candidate School.

outer envelope – calculated volume inside the published system periphery allowing hyperspace cruise and transition.

overhead – ceiling in a spaceship, without a room directly above.

PhD – Doctor of Philosophy; the most advanced degree in a field.

ppm – parts per million.

PR – public relations.

PSS – ship prefix, Paradiso Space Ship.

red team – attacker in a war game exercise.

R&R – Rest and Recuperation.

SM – CSF decoration, Science Medal.

SMH – Sigurdsen Military Hospital.

section – half of a division; in CSF, two ships.

squadron – group of ships under one command; in CSF, eight ships.

SSN – ship prefix, Samaran Space Navy.

STO – Senior Tactical Officer.

system periphery – published boundary inside which hyperspace cruise and transition are dangerous to the ship.

topside – cylinder(s) on a ship containing officer's quarters and command & control areas like the bridge, CIC, etc.

TNS – ship prefix, Tenerife Navy Ship.

UCS – Unarmed Combat School.

UJ – University of Jablonka.

VA – CSF decoration, Victorious Action ribbon.

VR – virtual reality.

XO – Executive Officer, First Officer.

zero-g – completely weightless; in free fall.

CAMPBELL: THE PROBLEM WITH BLISS

Made in the USA
Columbia, SC
19 December 2021

52142188R00096